Roas'nears, Rabbit Toback'r, & Rosebud Salve

Faye Brown
Illustrations by Trillie Brown

 SEVGO PRESS
PUBLISHERS
NORTHPORT, ALABAMA

Mrs. Brown is available for speaking engagements and autographing sessions. You may contact the author for appointments by telephone (205) 371-6316, or by mail at the following address:

Mrs. Faye Brown
Rt. 2, Box 440
Moundville, AL 35474

SEVGO Press titles are available at quantity discounts for sales promotions, premiums or fund raising. For information write to: Publisher, SEVGO Press, 1955 - 22nd St., Northport, AL 35476.

FIRST PRINTING • JULY 1992
ISBN 0-943487-39-0

PRINTED IN THE UNITED STATES OF AMERICA
SEVGO PRESS, 1955 – 22nd STREET, NORTHPORT AL 35476

Dedication

With Great Love and Appreciation

To my siblings: Frances, Bill, Sue, Betty, Trillie, Doug, and Ray. And to the memory of Little Robert and Donald. To these whose love and laughter insulated me against the Depression's hard times, inscribing fun stories upon my heart. Their continued love and encouragement today inspires me to keep pulling forth the tales and transposing them onto paper for you.

I have reached deep into the recesses of my heart to pull up these stories from the Great Depression for you, triggering my funny bone with the reaching. In the pulling I have also, from time-to-time, caught up a bit of fantasy. For in the tapestry of my life the real and imagined are only a thought, a pencil stroke apart. And added to my telling, you — my family, friends, and faithful readers — you've added your memories to embroider some gold around the edges of *Roas'nears, Rabbit Toback'r, and Rosebud Salve.*

Faye Brown

Thankee . . .

To John Seymour, my publisher, who keeps believing in my "stuff."

To John Cameron, the printer who keeps printing and assembling my books.

To Sherry Simon and her successor at SEVGO Press, Pamela Channell, who put up with me and see to it that the stores promptly receive my work.

To Trillie Brown, my dear sister, who keeps tolerating my mind changes and beautifully illustrating my writings.

To Joe, my husband of 36 years, who keeps helping me mail out my stuff and who keeps being patient even though the entire house is hidden underneath the clutter.

And most of all to You, my faithful readers, who keep telling me how much you enjoy my stories.

And most importantly, to Jesus Christ, my Creator and my Redeemer, who gave me life, who permitted me to experience these great times, and who continues giving me the opportunity to share these stories with you.

Contents

Hold Yer Horses . . .

Roas'nears, Rabbit Toback'r, and Rosebud Salve deserve much credit for my salvation during the Great Depression. The wharf rats'd get our cornbread makings, the foxes'd steal our chance of chicken and dumplings, and the canned vegetables'd play out.

But once we got that first skimpy grabeling of Irish 'taters and picking of English peas—once that happened, before we could say "Jack Robinson" we were saved by way of the sweet corn in the garden.

With roas'nears "in" we'd eat like kings, fatten ourselves up again. Gather a big arm load of the milky ears for creamed corn or corn - on - the - cob ever noontime and supper meal for months. Roas'nears was even a rare treat for Sunday breakfast.

The thing that kept me going while performing the awful chores back then—cleaning out a chicken house, picking velvet beans, or slopping the hogs—the goal that drew me onward was Bill's promise that I could sneak under the house with him later while he smoked a little rabbit toback'r. Just watching him puff that rabbit toback'r colby was like lightnin' a "far" under me; it'd git me going agin.

Life's knocks were hard on us. There'uz maddogs to look out for, hornets a'stangin' us, risin's (boils) on our bodies, and rusty nails always a'stickin' in our feet, threatening us with lockjaw. And you sure as shootin' better not get any dew in a sore during dog days. There weren't much you could take stock in, but you **could** depend on that Rosebud Salve.

Just to know that Mama had a little tin of the pink, fragrant life-preserving balm almost made it worthwhile getting a bad sore or a bee sting when I was a kid. Just a little smear was a cure-all for whatever ailed ye.

Why, I do believe if I'd had a little Rosebud Salve to spread on my sore finger tips months back, and a bait of fresh roas'nears outta Mama's garden, and maybe even a little puff offen a rabbit toback'r colby under the back porch with Bill—if I had had those life-extending, rejuvenating treats from childhood while I've been trying to get this *Roas'nears, Rabbit Toback'r, and Rosebud Salve* book done to a gnat's hair, why I do believe I'd have had this great volume in your hands much sooner. But hold yer horses 'cause good stuff's coming yer way d'rectly! Have yerself a time!

If You Were
Hatched after 1945

If you were unlucky enough to be hatched after 1945 many wonderful sights, sounds, smells, and tastes are probably foreign to you. You probably do not recall the wonderful thrill of licking a BB Bat, a heavenly candy that you bargained for, swapping a hen egg for it at the rolling store along the dusty country road. You most likely have never relished popcorn balls or molasses taffy made by you and your siblings on a cold winter's night out in the freezing kitchen.

It is plausible that you have never eaten the heart out of a watermelon with your bare hands. You have never eaten a melon thusly that you found growing "volunteer" in the cotton patch in late September if you were hatched, as my folks sometimes referred to my birth, if you came out of the shell after 1945.   And you've missed the delicious aroma of ripe muscadines, fox grapes, or persimmons after frost.   The sheer ecstasy of realizing you're walking in the woods near one of the latter wild delicacies has presumably never motivated you to break into a run.

If the stork brought you after WWII ended, there's a good chance you've never had chicken 'n dumplings with a chicken's foot cooked therein, or eaten the north end of a chicken flying south. Your grandmother may never have called you to the table and served up a plate of poke salat, or green onions scrambled with eggs, or kraut that she has, that very day, finished fermenting in a crock.

Or, perhaps greater than those, you missed out on enjoying freshly-churned butter spread onto hot cornbread that your great aunt cooked in an ancient dutch oven atop a pile of hot coals on her hearth. Or butter applied liberally onto a steaming sweet potato that someone had just pulled from the ashes in the fireplace. The only thing that could possibly have been a greater loss for you is not ever enjoying a blackberry pie while you still had chiggers in your 'nabel to prove that you'd helped pick the berries.

You "Johnny-come-latelys" have come up on the short end of the stick on smells as well as tastes. Who among you have felt intoxicated over the smell of hams and sausages curing in the smokehouse, each of them inhaling days and nights of hickory smoke? Or the incense wafting heavenward when sorghum and ribbon cane was being turned into 'lasses down by the creek in the fall? Granny's hominy shedding its skin amidst the bag of ash lye in the black iron pot is one smell I'm sorry you didn't catch. And I'd not swap the memory of brunswick stew a-simmering under the mulberry tree at Granny's on the Fourth of July for all the gourmet meals on five continents. But I will concede that I could have lived without the lingering smell of the wool rags and wisps of my own hair a-burning in a late afternoon's gnat smoke.

There is an almost endless list of unusual experiences that you young whippersnappers skipped. Who among you can say they shot marbles during school recess, as soon as they returned from the outhouse down in the bushes? Or jumped "hot peas?" Or swung out of the barn loft on a grass rope? Found a hen's nest that the old dominecker had "stolen" down in the woods?

Don't I have a well-founded reason to

believe you never made a whistle from the reeds along the creek bank? Took a nap on a bale of cotton piled on the front porch? Wore a dress made from a feed sack? Or bloomers that read "Self-Rising" on them? I suspect you also missed pulling the pulley-bone when the preachers came to dinner? And you young boys have never swam in your birthday suit down in the mill pond when no one of the opposite sex was around.

The crowing of a rooster will be remembered as an outstanding sound only by those of us born before Harry Truman became President of the United States of America. That and the clucking of the setting hen as she led her little biddies around the yard, protecting the baby chicks from the old lazy squirrel dog and from the chicken hawks who swooped down occasionally.

You of the younger generation will not cherish the memory of "Lum and Abner" on the neighbor's radio, because your family could not afford a battery-powered radio of their own. You were the ones who had to go outside and wait beside the road for the school bus; not us — we could wait inside the house and hear the school bus whining for miles. It was practically the only vehicle which traveled our country roads. Well, there WAS the letter carrier who came around noon every day except Sunday; we of the older generation knew the sound of his car as well.

It has been my finding that folks who came

along after the forties don't consider a soothing lullaby the same as I — katydids a-singing, crickets a-chirping, hoot owls a-screeching, or bob cats a-screaming up in the hills. They can't even mimic the sounds that are old hat to us: calling cows from the pasture when it was time to milk, calling pigs to the trough when you brought down the slop, calling the chickens while you stood in the back yard shelling a few ears of corn for their supper.

What a shame, what a shame! So many wonderful sights, sounds, smells, and tastes of my days are completely alien to you if you came along after 1945. Oh, your modern parents probably acknowledged that you were "born" instead of shyly saying you were "hatched." But you are to be pitied, perhaps the most because you never knew the sheer ecstasy of hearing the dinner bell ring and knowing you could knock-off the hoeing in the cotton patch and hurry to enjoy one of Mama's vegetable dinners, a heavenly meal cooked on the old wood stove.

It May Be Another Eating Peas With a Knife Year

The year has dawned dark with signs of a deeping recession. It makes me wonder if soon folks won't be reverting to the Great Depression motto: "Use it up, wear it out; make it do, or do without." In other words, all signs are pointing to another *Eating - Peas - With - a - Knife* year.

My great Aunt Beck's daughter, Aunt Velma as we called her, believed in sharing with others regardless of hard times. Living, as she did, just below Hannah Church, where we walked to Sunday School and preaching when I was a wee tot, put me on the receiving end of her generosity many times. One day's impromptu dinner invitation stands out in my mind.

There we were — a whole passel of folks besides my Mama and Daddy and their seven younguns at the time — all heading to Aunt Velma's well for a dipper of good cold water and, at her insistence, trudging down the good woman's dogtrot for dinner after Sunday church.

Of course the grownups got first dibs on the food so they sat around the long table in the good smelling kitchen. But being the kind soul she was Aunt Velma wouldn't hear of letting us hungry kiddos wait until a *second table* could be served. Instead she scrounged up all the chipped or tin plates on the hill and served us promptly.

We sat on the back steps enjoying our chicken drumsticks, our cornbread, our corn - on - the - cob. Everything went smoothly while we ate our *finger foods*, if you please. But then we came to the pile of peas on our plates.

"Aunt Velma", I called, "we'd sure thankee fer some forks to eat our peas with." The robust lady appeared quickly, passing out tableknives, saying, "I'm sorry younguns, I'm fresh outta forks but peas are *really* made to be et with a knife, anyway." And while she passed out knives she repeated a little folk ditty.

> *I eat my peas with honey,*
> *I've done it all my life,*
> *It makes my peas taste funny*
> *But it sticks them to my knife.*

Balancing those peas on the slender blade of a knife and getting them into my mouth was one of the biggest challenges of my young life. But we kids had fun doing it, and with perseverance our stomachs were filled. The experience was just one example of how we learned to make - do with what we had during the Depression.

I recently flipped through a magazine for ritzy home entertaining. It boldly proclaimed that the etiquette powers - that - be had decided it was OK to set a dinner table with one antique china plate of each pattern. Or to put it like I grew up hearing, to "have a dukesmixture, or use your odds and ends, to make out with whatever you've got."

Mama always was a pacesetter, fifty years before her time with example and language. Only difference being, the odd plates Mama set our table with came not from hunting in antique stores. They were remnants of cheap sets once owned by my folks or their ancestors.

Mama's and Daddy's first set of dishes came with the kitchen cabinet purchased at their marriage; the entire kit and caboodle, including the built - in flour bin and sifter, cost the newlyweds thirty-two dollars. Of course after having two houses completly destroyed by tornadoes there were few dishes left intact.

They added to their china and crystal

gradually, whenever the Crystal Oat packages had little Depression glass dishes inside. Along the route somewhere we had acquired a few tin plates as well; these came in handy for little kids learning to eat before Tommy Tippee or Tupperware invented plastic ones. And we set the table three times daily with what we had, never having a thought — during the Depression — that we needed to purchase an all - alike, complete set of dishes.

We also made out with oddlot *silverware,* or *knives and forks* as we called it back then. Some of our *sterling* was really tin; if someone forgot and left a big spoon in the creamed corn when it was tucked underneath the tablecloth in the middle of the table after dinner on a hot summer day — well, when Mama left the field early to fix supper she'd find that the spoon had turned green in the corn, ruining the supper. Of course it was immediately dashed into the slop bucket for the pigs to enjoy. And the tin spoon caused someone to hurriedly gather fresh roas'nears for supper.

My young daughter - in - law was excited about having in her hope chest a set of pint fruit jars, with handles, for teaglasses. Maybe this is a good sign. Perhaps the young **could** adjust to using Granny's snuff glasses for crystal like Mama did. Or to using jelly glasses like Joe and I did after we married almost four decades back.

Pots and pans were passed from one generation to the next when times were hard. The iron skillets, the bakers, the huge pots with handles in which mamas cooked black - eyed peas they had grown and threshed — cooked them over the fireplace to save on stovewood. These useful family members might come out of the antique corner and make a comeback if the recession deepens into a depression.

And when the enamel chips off of boilers, as in years past, today's young couples may learn to search hardware stores for mendits to repair the leaks in the pans instead of quickly shuffling them into the garbage and heading to the department store with their plastic money.

And, who is to predict, but if folks in high density population areas continue to lose their jobs they just might head back to the rural lands which are now lying waste and plant a big patch of black - eyed peas. They might dig themselves a well of water, run into town and buy a length of rope, a water bucket, and a dipper.

Finding the depression more than they can handle alone, they might get right with God and be at church on Sunday morning. They might even invite neighbors home after church for a dipper of cold water from their bucket at the well. And during a meal together — if there weren't enough forks to go around who would mind — with their pull - togetherness and neighborly love intact. Come to think of it, it just might not be such a bad thing, after all, if this turned out to be another *Eating - Peas - With - A - Knife* year.

Bathing In A No. 3 Tub
Behind The Wood Stove

The mercury outside my door had dipped to zero and the windchill, according to the meteorologist's report, was well 35 below. But I was lucky: my heat pump was working overtime to keep me regulated at a pleasant 75 degrees. And then came bath time. Even with the electric heater in the bathroom wall pushing the air up to 90, I still had trouble coaxing myself out of the warm jogging suit to sit in a bathtub.

My mind raced backwards to my childhood: Saturday night bathing behind the wood stove, out in the kitchen come wintertime. Cold water, drawn from the well was first put into the tub. Additional water was heated in the stove's built - on hot water tank called a reservoir, or else the water was heated in iron kettles, pots, and pans on the stove while the hot bread was cooked for the evening meal.

After supper was finished and the dishes washed and put away, the bathing ritual began. Some households began with the oldest and worked down, with the youngest child having to bath last, in the tub of dirty water. We began with the youngest and worked up, partially, I think, because bedtime came earliest for the youngest.

But regardless of the order in which the bathing cycle was approached, when it fell my turn to enter the kitchen alone and remove my out'n (flannel) petticoat and floursack bloomers I knew definitely I lived in America and not in Finland. Bathing in a cold No. 3 washtub behind Mama's kitchen stove in a tenant farming house on Mr. Jonah's place left no doubt about me possibly bathing in a Finnish sauna. That is, unless the sauna process had been reversed and I was getting the dip in the icy lake or snow as a first step.

You see, I've read that the first step in a Finnish bath is to sit in a bathhouse where the steam — sometimes from water splashed onto hot rocks where the temperature reaches 175-225 degrees. And sitting awkwardly — half in, half out of a galvanized tub — in a kitchen that is only about 30 degrees itself with a steady wind cruising through the large cracks — well, suffice it to say that you'd never start sweating like they do in the Finnish saunas.

But I suppose you could compare the drying off with a rough guano - sack towel to the scrubbing of feet skin with a pumice stone which I've read they do following a sweating session in a sauna bath, Finland style. Their baths are also long drawn - out affairs; I assure you I could be in and out of Mama's wash tub on a freezing night before you could say "Jack Robinson." Maybe almost as fast as Ole Jake moved one night, just after finishing his tub bath.

Now the way I heard Daddy and the menfolk out at the woodpile telling it — while I was hidden underneath the hedge, playing hide 'n seek. Well, they told it this way: Old Jake had his bathing tub **in front of** the kitchen stove one night, not behind it, as was usual. As he, shivering and shaking, climbed outta the tub and bent over for his guano - sack towel, he forgot just how close he was to the stove. The fat feller let out a deafening scream; his wife Liza Jane ran to investigate. She found his dear back side clearly branded — with the words from the stove door:

Home Comfort!

Summertime bathing, when I was a kid, differed from wintertime. Since heating for the water then came from the sun's rays, often every washtub we owned — two, three, depending on how many had sprung leaks — often every tub was filled with water out near the well, or down at the spring, during the dinner hour on every single day, not just Saturdays.

Then come quitting time in the fields, we'd rush to complete chores and head for the tubs which we then moved behind the smokehouse, or made sure they were screened by thick bushes down at the spring. We'd especially hurry to bathe the field dust from ourselves if we were headed to a protracted meeting at church that night.

However, if we planned to play outside in the dusty yard catching June bugs and lightning bugs or playing ante - over with the string ball— if we planned to do this after supper then the bathing would wait until last. And then it'd be done under the cover of darkness, sometimes out in the middle of the yard since we had no close neighbors.

And, according to the menfolk I overheard that day discussing Ole Jake's bathing calamities—according to Daddy summertime bathing back in those days could be almost as hazardous as in the wintertime. Well, seems it was only at the nagging of his wife that big, 300 lb. Jake ever bathed in a No. 3 tub at all. But one year Liza Jane insisted he spruce up for the kinfolks who were coming on the 4th of July.

Well, Jake stripped off under the cover of dusty dark out in the middle of the backyard, and decided to just sorta sit on the tub's rim, with his feet down on the ground. He splashed water on himself and applied a lot of his wife's lye soap, the brown slimy kind. Pretty soon he got all slippery and his big backside began to slide down into the tub. Before he realized it he was touching the bottom of the tub.

About this time Jake heard a commotion coming up the lane. There was a cowbell ringing: "Had he forgotten to put Ole Bossy into the lot?" Next he heard a fox horn, then plow shares being beaten. It dawned on him! The young boys were out serenading for the Fourth and they were nearing the barn - lot!

Jake commenced to struggle to get out of the tub; the harder he tried the more tightly he became stuck. Just as the boys approached him he gave one last desperate surge. He flung himself over, tub and all, and went scrambling and clawing around the corner of the smokehouse, like a giant sea turtle, crawling, propelling himself with both hands and feet while the tub was borne high up in the air, stuck to his backside.

I thought my Daddy and the other men at the woodpile that day would just keel over laughing at their remembrance of seeing Ole Jake when they were young, pranking boys. "Him runnin' on all - fours," they hollered, "and the No. 3 tub 'a - pouring its water down from his fat fanny."

Then my Daddy confessed to the risk that bathing had once posed to his own life; a danger brought about by the use of Granny's lye soap when there'd been no store - bought. He testified concerning his Ma's syrupy red torture, "It'll sure take yer hide, even after you've done a heap o'rinsing."

Actually the only kind of cleanliness that was enjoyable long ago was that achieved through summertime bathing — wading, splashing, swimming, diving from vines in trees — through contact with water down at the creek, mind you. Or that brief ritual known as *washing your feet* which was required nightly, except on bath nights. Feet were washed up on the back porch during hot summers. And when shoes were removed on freezing nights, feet were washed in basins by the fireside before one could retire for the night.

And, of course, there was the painless washing of one's hands and face — and combing of one's hair — which was accomplished at the backporch shelf in summers and at a stand in the kitchen during winters. This latter was required before every mealtime at our home, and at most other homes in our neighborhood.

Yep, many of my generation are prone to forget. In these days when we can keep our bodies clean by means of hot tubs, in home saunas, or nice hot showers — and all within the confines of private, comfortable surroundings — we sometimes forget how lucky we are.

In order to remain properly thankful we should not erase the memories of the Sat'dy nite bathing in a No. 3 tub behind the wood stove on a freezing night. It made us want to do like a woman I heard of recently. When questioned by the home health nurse as to whether or not she bathed daily she replied, "Well, no ma'ms, I don't. I don't have no bathtub — but most nights I does rags down my parts."

I Allez Had Pine Rasum On My Back Side

I allez (always) had pine rasum (resin) on my backside as a young'un. I was not a standout in that however. Not during the Great Depression. Not when wood - burning cook stoves and fireplaces were the only way folks filled their bellies and warmed their toes.

Spending a big chunk of one's day steadying a log for sawing was a normal part of most kids' lives back then. And so I sat. Sat with my younger siblings a - straddle uf a downed pine tree. Sat through chilly wintry afternoons and frigid Sat'dy mornings. Sat shivering, freezing, while Daddy and my big brother sweated, pulling that old crosscut back and forth. Sat glued. Glued to the log by sheer willpower and the pine rasum on my backside.

Some of our long - ago neighbors stacked their wood head high in late summers. We were not so blessed. After the crops were laid by our Daddy walked the dusty roads, selling insurance or fruit trees, trying to make a thin dime to keep our heads above the water. And we younguns picked punctured squares out of the cotton patch, trying to soften the boll weevils' blow. Thus the arrival of cold weather found us struggling. Struggling daily, hourly, to maintain enough wood for cornbread cooking in the kitchen and thawing out bodies in the front room. Found me always struggling to keep rasum off my backside.

My brother Bill, forced quickly to mature beyond his years, rushed on short winter afternoons from the school bus, quickly changed into his over - patched overalls. Eating a cold 'tater as he ran he soon had a couple 'o fresh cut pines snaked into the yard, with Old Frank's help and a chain. Meanwhile Mama'd issue her warning, "Girls, gobble down your sugar - biscuit and get into your ever'day clothes. And bundle up good with your old coats and flour sack head rags. Your Daddy'll be coming from the barn for sawing any minute now!"

When Mama directed us into old clothes we knew it didn't matter if smudges of the pine sap got onto us. Saturated us as it seeped from the cut tree while we sat steadying a log for sawing into stovewood lengths. It mattered not to Mama if the pine rasum got onto my ever'day garments as the tree bled where its limbs had been severed by Bill's quick ax. Or at least Mama understood about the old things and didn't scold.

One reason Mama suffered patiently through washing old clothes with pine rasum on their backsides was because she liked having pine stovewood. It burned quickly, especially if the log was dry — which ours seldom was. But pine heated the stove top and oven quickly for meals.

Pine performed the same fast - heating job as firewood and was sometimes used there — most often as small, filler sticks for quick starts. However, hickory and oaks were standbys for long lasting back sticks in the fireplace; in addition to lasting a longer time they didn't pop like pine. The rich resin of the pine — the part of it that didn't stick onto the back of my dresses and my naked, chapped legs — the pine rasum in the wood often caused little explosions during the fuel's burning. This resulted in bits of fire being popped dangerously onto the wooden floor or the nearby churn rag. Pine definitely couldn't be used in the fireplace near bedtime or when the fire was not attended.

Yep, Mama endured pine rasum on our old clothes because she liked pine stovewood. But let

me or my siblings come - up with any rasum
adhered to a Sunday - go - to - meetin' or a
knock - about, or even a school garment and we
were *in dutch*, in *uh heap o trouble*, if you please.

For, you see, patience grew short after
reminders were given — time and again — given
repeatedly before any chores which involved the
risk of pine rasum. Why, Mama'd remember to
admonish daily, "Nonie, jerk on these patched
overalls. And, mind you, take off that good
blouse. Tottin' in that stovewood's liab'l'st ruin it,
what with the splinters, pine rasum 'n all."

Despite the frequent warnings, however,
when my elders were caught up with Sunday -
dinner - company, I sometimes grew lax on the
important rules I knew. I kept on my Sunday
dress and rushed into the woods to climb and
swing out young pine trees. Or I scampered, nice
clothes on, with the preacher's kids out to the
pine - slabbed see - saw balanced atop Daddy's
chopping block. My being hospitable won
Mama's approval; having a big glob of rasum
from the see - saw or the rough seat of the plow -
line swing, having the rasum attached to my good
garments brought out Mama's other side.

Some of the pine rasum might never have
reached my backside long ago if we'd been
equipped like a few of our neighbors. Some of
their woodpiles boasted a rack for holding logs in
place for the sawing process. Two rough 2 x 4's

or two small saplings stuck into the earth, about hip - high. Then a latch fell across the top to secure a felled tree for sawing. Nothing really difficult to construct. Looking back a half - century later, I can only conclude that my Daddy preferred the laughter — and the grumbling betimes of his kiddoes out there straddling the pine - rasum - dabbed logs. Preferred live - holders to constructing himself such a log - holding device.

When wood was needed strong Bill would tug a felled pine tree atop a large round length of log — a gigantic back stick — if you please. Daddy'd walk up about then, whistle, and say, "Hop on, Squire Skimp." Immediately we kids jumped astride the log, be it oak or be it pine, sticky with rasum.

For the drawn - out chore of zipping the saw back and forth energetic Bill just bent his strong back up and down. Daddy, however — middle - aged when even his first of ten kids had been born — my aging Daddy most always sawed from a kneeling position. There he, weary from his labors, would rest one knee of his worn thin pants on the cold sod and the rasum - y wood chips.

As the men pulled back and forth, back and forth zip, zip, zip — the little pile of sawdust underneath the log began to grow. One by one, the lengths of pine were dismembered from the log and fell with a heart - warming thud to the ground.

Once the work began it wasn't long before the saw started to move sluggishly, kept from its rounds by the pesky pine rasum, the sticky sap of the pine trees. So occasionally the sawers would pause. Daddy'd pick up his little *dope bottle* (an old Coca-Cola bottle), sling a few drops of its kerosene through the pine - straw - bristled - stopper and onto the saw. This would cut through the glue, the resin. Soon they'd be zipping rhythmically once again.

It made me feel grown - up when Daddy couldn't help saw and I was drafted to take his place on one end of the crosscut. Bill'd usually grumble, however, talking about how I just "lay down on the saw," "make it wobble," or "can't pull through hot butter."

As Daddy sawed he sometimes whistled. And we kids often sang, "Row, row, row your boat" in rounds. That is, we would sing unless we had dislodged a drying lump of the pine rasum and decided to try to chew it. In which case we would be concentrating on pulling, raking, jerking, scraping — trying to get the rasum to dislodge from our teeth.

Sometimes it seemed that before you could say "Jack Robinson" the wood would be sawed, ready for Bill or Daddy to split into small sticks for the stove. Or medium and small sticks of firewood would be waiting for totting to the front room.   And, when I attempted to arise in celebration, I'd discover that I was stuck fast. It was never a surprise, not really. Because from a wee tot I **allez, allez** had pine rasun on my back side.

'Whoopee' — Whoopees Are In Again

I sat in the center court of a shopping mall, moaning over my aching feet clad in high heels and panty hose that kept working up, driving me batty. As I paused thusly, sipping a little caffeine and dreaming of my comfy socks back home, my eyes fell on a troop of eloquent ladies whose every movement whispered "sophistication, fashion mongers."

My eyes traveled from their jewelry to their silk crepe dresses/slacks and then stopped, abruptly, at their feet. They all sported flat shoes and **white socks**. Unable to restrain myself in that moment of realized liberation I stood and shouted for all the world to hear, **"Whoopee!** whoopees are *in* again!"

It took me back to my childhood, to my high school days when white cotton anklets with turn - down tops were fashionable with all garments. Even the most style conscious — those lucky girls who possessed poodle skirts — wore the comfortable white Bobby Socks with their skirts and dresses. Coupled with saddle oxfords or penny loafers the socks went to school, to ball games, to sock hops, to church . . . you name it; the anklets were hot fashion attire.

Now my family was too poor for me to ever sport one of the poodle skirts and they had a tough time getting me an el cheapo pair of saddle oxfords from the Sears - Roebuck cattylog, but I did have white socks — albeit usually only one pair at a time — and I grew up enjoying their comfort.

I could empathize with my Aunt Essie, who at 40 years old was still a *special child*. I felt with her when she resisted her Mama's efforts to make her wear long cotton stocking with garters. She'd beg, "Aw, Maw, jest let me wear some whoopees." Essie's name for the comfortable anklets, Webster tells me, means to express exuberance, or, a loud yell of jubilation. Now I doubt that Essie ever knew the meaning of the word but it was very appropriate since she and I were alike in hating to wear cotton stockings with garters and alike in our love for whoopees.

Keeping a pair of whoopees to wear to school each day was a problem for me and my siblings. Sometimes as the turnip greens simmered on the cookstove on winter nights a pan containing water, lye soap, and dirty white socks might also be found alongside, boiling. And every night just after supper we could be found scrubbing our one good pair of socks at the washpan in the kitchen. We then hung them on chair rungs near the fireplace where they soaked up the last heat from the dying fire to, hopefully, be dried for wearing the following morning.

Being made of one hundred percent cotton the socks, seemingly, acquired holes in the heels almost overnight. So we learned, my brothers included, at an early age to mend our socks. Mama taught us how to put something (a glass, or in years after electricity, a *blown* light bulb), how to insert the hard object into the sock underneath the worn spot. And then we learned how to take needle and thread and sew back and forth — reweaving, if you please — until the sock had a new heel intact. (When I took Home Economics in high school the darning of socks was also one of the main things that was emphasized and I had to learn to do it so perfectly that one could not tell the sock had ever been torn.)

Mama assures me that the issue of a

comfortable and stylish covering for the foot and leg is one that has been around for many years. She remembers that as a child before WWI she had to wear either black or dark brown ribbed stockings. They were secured above her knees with elastic garters. According to her it was a "pain in the neck" trying to keep the garter rolled tight enough to keep the stockings from slipping down during games at school or work at home.

Mama said she never had a love for the long cotton stockings even though she, when grown, helped make them in a stocking factory in Kaulton, sort of the west end of Tuscaloosa, Alabama. She admitted, however, that if the stockings "had to be" then the factory was a great improvement over the spinning wheel for thread making and the hand knitting of the stockings that my Granny Porter had done for her big brood.

Mama envied girls and ladies who could afford fancy *lyle* stockings which were **the thing** for dress - up when she was small. And she felt quite important sporting the silk stockings with seams and decorations in the back which came into vogue when she was a pretty young lady, proud to have a job and able to purchase them. But even the silk stockings had to be *held up* over the knee with an elastic band, or garter, that encircled the leg.

That is, the stockings were kept over the knee until the 20s when, for a time, it became fashionable to roll them down and show the knees. Mama still sings a folk song, of unknown origin, that made it's rounds back then and went something like this:

Don't let folks tell you that it's shocking
When boys whisper 'bout your stockings—
Roll 'em girls, roll 'em,
Go ahead and roll 'em,
Roll 'em down
And show your pretty knees.

Nylon stockings hit the market in 1938 when I was just a wee chap but I didn't realize it for a long time. In fact, nylons had barely made their impact when WWII came along and caused all nylon to be routed for the production of parachutes and other military fabrics. However, when the war was over and stockings once more began to be manufactured from nylon fabric a mad frenzy erupted among ladies seeking to own nylon stockings, according to old newspaper accounts. The *Borax Review* article listed headlines that appeared around the country such as "Thousands Storm Counters for Nylons," and "Eight Girls Lose Homes in Fire; Nylons Saved." There was even a picture of a lady sitting on the street curb putting on her new nylons because she couldn't wait to wear them.

Stockings have undergone many great improvements through the years. As a teenager wearing my first few pairs of nylons, when getting a *run* was catastrophic, the change from garters to a garter belt was a terrific help. The belt made it easier to keep seams of stockings straight down the back of my legs and kept me from punching so many holes in my nylons, trying to straighten them.

Then the advent of stockings without seams opened a whole new era for many of us ladies. However, nothing short of the invention of fire came as close to revolutionizing the lives of women as did the advent of panty hose.

But even with all the innovations in panty hose — the varied lengths, shapes, sizes, fabrics, control tops vs loose tops, regular vs queen sizes vs Big Mamas — in spite of the flexibility available something is still lacking. Even with all the choices a pair of panty hose can never, in my eyes, come close to matching the comfort of a pair of cotton anklets which do not bind the leg, nor twist, nor ride up after a few hours. Good comfortable socks, if you please, which absorb perspiration and let your feet breathe easily. And so, recently while I sat in the mall suffering from *panty - hose contortionitis* — while I sat there and spied the stylish ladies all decked out in their silks and wearing white cotton socks it was only fitting that my mind should flash back to the comfort that I and my dear Aunt Essie enjoyed when I was a child. Only proper that in that moment I should jump to my feet and shout, for myself and all

womankind,   **"Whoopee!**   Whoopees   are   *in*
again!"

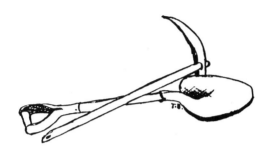

Work On The WPA:
A Gravy Train For Daddy

Daddy regarded the opportunity to work on the WPA just like a "gravy train; manna from heaven," so to speak. Not much wonder considering that he could make "a - buck - 'n - a - quarter or a - buck - 'n - a - half" in just one day. And that he could, in turn, buy a twenty - four pound sack of flour for just fifty cents. It meant the road job given Daddy between crop times in the late 30s translated into a lot of biscuits for our family that we would otherwise have gone without.

The Works Progress Administration, established in 1935 as part of President

Roosevelt's New Deal, employed an average of 2,000,000 workers annually between 1935 and 1941. I am aware that it cost the federal government a great amount of money to finance this and other emergency measures to give work to the unemployed and that this is debatable even today as the beginning of our unbelievable national debt.

But at that time in our depressed economy when a job in the private sector was almost impossible to obtain — ours was just one of millions of families the WPA kept from possible starvation.

Working in a rural area of Pickens County, Alabama, Daddy's job often meant a back - breaking day's work with a shovel or a pick. The efforts of his group to stop erosion on the shoulders of the gravel road over toward's Granny's house, to restore the foundation dirt that had been washed from underneath the wooden bridge up on Big Hill, and to build a new bridge at the cutoff, near Jeff's place, so folks could get to the gristmill better — these public road maintenance labors helped fulfill the initial objectives of the program.

And when Daddy came home exhausted at night, he came with pride. He was proud that on Saturday he'd be able to drive the team into town to buy flour, sugar, and some shoes for the baby's feet. And proud that he'd given an honest day's work in return — work to help out his community, his county, his country.

The WPA also created work for artists, writers, actors, and musicians, I have heard. In fact, I talked just recently with a lady who has done research in many libraries, making use of the stories and documents recorded by the writers during the WPA program. According to her, they often recorded stories of the sad predicament of the 'pore folks'.

Jeb told me a few days ago that he worked for the WPA back then. Worked in a fair - sized town, though; not a rural area like Daddy did. Said he and hundreds of others like him helped sanitize the world; they built 'johns' throughout America. I forgot to ask him if his job fell under the 'artists' category.

Yep, they helped to transform the towns and cities from a mass of folks hiding behind bushes into nice "two - seaters," he said. Even, in some instances, "two big seats and a small 'un for the kiddoes." And, just like those $500.00 toilet seats put into U.S. Government jet planes in the 1980s, just like that the government gave the folks strict specifications for the outhouses. Had to have so many square feet of space for each occupant and things like that. "Building privies was the way I got my start in life. First job I got just outta high school," Jeb 'lowed. "Be a fine b'ginnin' fer young folks t'day, I reck'n."

A lot of other young men got their start in the CCCs back then. Boys from needy families who were seventeen or older, or who could be "slid under the wire fer seventeen," were actually the ones who launched the New Deal relief program in 1933. President Roosevelt's first term in office saw these unemployed young men recruited into a civilian army called the Civilian Conservation Corps.

Apt as not if you'll take time to investigate the area where you now reside within the United States you'll be able to locate some nearby benefits from the labors of the CCC boys who conserved and developed our national resources. They helped build bridges, roads, cabins, lakes, and national parks. And they helped refine national forests across our land.

Living in Moundville, Alabama with its beautiful state park makes me daily appreciate the efforts of these workers. Two friends of mine recently reminded me that it was the CCCs who excavated the mounds, who unearthed the evidence of the Mississippian Indians which may today be viewed in the Mound State Museum. They also transformed the rough terrain into the beautiful state park that it is today. Many state and national parks across our great United States were thusly transformed by the boys.

My friend, Mr. Bob Rogers, said he joined the group at age nineteen. Mr. Odis Tucker, however, was "sneaked in a little before the seventeen - year - limit by a welfare worker" who sensed the great need for Odis to become a provider of bread for his parents and siblings. In the beginning Odis' salary was thirty dollars per month. Twenty - five was sent home to his family; five dollars was his for toiletries, stamps to write home with, and cash for courting. Later Odis' pay rose to thirty - five dollars per month and was divided twenty - two/eight.

But, Odis reflected recently with a laugh, the "courtin' budget didn't need to be fat." There wasn't much to do in the small town of Moundville in the 30s, plus the CCC boys were viewed with suspicion by the townfolks .

Being faithful at the local churches — which was one thing expected of the recruits by their superiors — well, church attendance was the only way to win adults' confidence and be allowed to escort one of their daughters to a high school basketball game.

Odis affirmed that without the money he provided, his family would have eaten cornbread for breakfast instead of biscuits. And Bob added, "Whooo — if it hadn't been for the money I sent, my family just couldn't have made it."

Food was plentiful and delicious in the CCC camps, even feasts compared to the sparse depression meals that most of the boys were accustomed to at home. They had chickens aplenty; fact is the camps often raised their own chickens for meat and eggs. They also had good vegetables, bologna, and occasionally had steak.

"On Sundays we had all the ice cream we could eat," my friend Odis recalls. "And watermelon cuttin's in the summertime."

Both of my Moundville neighbors felt the regimen of the camp — the exercise, strict rules, hard work, time for play, reveille, expectation of worship on Sunday, recognition for good conduct and leadership abilities — which was very similar to the military back then — both felt these were good for their lives. Mr. Odis laughingly agreed that it didn't scar his personality, not even when punished for something he didn't do; when another member of his group committed a No - No and the entire group had to miss scheduled visits home and spend the entire weekend painting chicken houses.

And, indeed the corps did prove to be very good training for many. It panned out a terrific foundation for the boys - turned - men when WW II broke out. They made wonderful soldiers in a short time. Many felt they owed a great debt of gratitude to their country for the help that had been given them and their families through the CCCs. So they gladly answered the call to duty; they sacrificed, they gave their strength, their devotion, and some even gave their lives.

Many of the CCC camps also provided an

opportunity for boys to further their education while in the camps. Local teachers often came to the camps late in the afternoons or early evenings and gave lessons for the boys. This layed the foundation for many of them to later become outstanding professional men — doctors, lawyers, preachers, and businessmen.

Yes, the Civilian Conservation Corps represented a way out of a pit for many poor families during the 30s. It was like being out in the wilderness with Moses, hungry, and having the Lord let the fat quails just walk up, daily, into the camp. And having the opportunity to work on, and receive wages from, the WPA was similar. It was, for my Daddy, like manna falling down from heaven or like a blessed gravy train pulling right up to our own front door.

A Trip To Jamaica or Just a Good Spring Tonic

Many of us are alike. 'Long about March - April we've run out of steam—survived the three-months - hype of the holidays and passed through the great - expectations - peak of the New Year only to have a lethargy set in. We're beset by an abnormal laziness or indifference to life that we have trouble putting our finger on.

Nowadays folks make expensive visits to specialists, to psychologists, or trips to the beach — all in an effort to dispel their apathy, their stupor. I wouldn't be surprised if all we really need, as Mama maintained every year when the sap began to rise, is simply a good spring tonic.

Years ago when a'body was bilious, puny, or whatever, there were home remedies or spring tonics in abundance to get them over the hump, without any sort of an expensive trip.

Millions in our neck of the woods made it through on sassafras tea. It could be had by simply going into the woods and digging roots from the sassafras, a tree of the laurel family. After the roots dried the bark therefrom was boiled and a liberal portion of the liquid was meted out to all family members. Some folks, however, boiled the entire roots for their medication. Still others insisted that roots from the red sassafras was better for you than those from the white tree.

An oddball bunch who once lived across the hollow from us believed in fever grass tea for their yearly pergative; a weed called fever grass was hunted and boiled for its potential bellyache.

Another tonic from plants, a Fall tonic however, one which I am happy to testify I averted, was prepared long ago by a Granny in Florida; Rabbit Tobacco Tea. According to her daughter, Alma Dean, who survived the concoction, you may prepare and serve in the following manner: Break up the rabbit tobacco twigs, cover with water and boil about twenty minutes. Drain off and sweeten the brew with either sugar or syrup. Drink a cup of it for three consecutive nights, skip three nights, then repeat

the process until you have consumed nine cups of
the bitter stuff. After you've had this "through" of
the tonic, you'll see an improvement in your
blood, also you will not be bothered with the
common cold. (I question whether one would be
around to be bothered with **anything** after
drinking that *remedy*.)

A spring tonic which veered from plants
was heard of in a settlement neighboring ours
years ago. The clan burned a deer's horn into
ashes every winter. Then they mixed the
powdered horn with honey and gave the helpless
kids a daily dose — if they happened to look a
little jaundiced in the springtime. I seriously doubt
that it could have been any worse than "the
round" of sulphur and molasses my Mama once
poured into my defenseless stomach.

I almost lost a friend in childhood; the girl's
parents made a drink for her out of yellow root
(they also kept some around to be chewed in case
one had a canker sore in their mouth). And two
fellers recently confessed to me that years ago
they were helped through their end - of - winter
slump with juice from boiled roots of the poke
salat plant. One of them said he was also cured
of the seven - year - itch by bathing in a tub of
juice from the same poke salat roots. Of course,
he had to be chased down and caught in the
process. The bath liquid "set me on fire and
warped me up," that is, it caused his skin to

initially break out in spotches and whelp up.

And then there were the more modern, up-to-date folks who'd give their last dime during the Great Depression for a bottle of Castor Oil to administer routinely along about breaking-up time (about the time the land was plowed with the break plow). Maybe the worst case of deception ever practiced by a mother came to light last year when someone told how their elder got the horrible oil down them after they had consumed "a bait" of something they should not have, say a "bait of green apples." She used the oil to make homemade mayonnaise and then prepared them delicious sandwiches using the dangerous spread.

Some believed in the brown *Carter's Little Liver Pills* in my early years. And untold numbers swore by *Black Draught*; which I feel was appropriately named since nothing could have tasted more like it was a drink straight from the gates of dark Hades. One friend shuddered that her mother kept a little cup of *Black Draught* heated on the back of the wood stove at all times; anyone who complained of a stomach ache, or any other ache for that matter, had to take a sip of the horrid stuff. It doesn't surprise me that this octogenarian friend never complains of her many ills today; the threat of Black Draught would teach even a fool to keep their mouth shut regarding their physical problems.

It mattered not how good we siblings were feeling come spring long ago, nor how much we pretended to be super when we were actually puny. There'd come a day when Mama'd line us up, one and all, and start making her diagnosis: "Nonie, you're plumb green around the gills. Bill, you look bilious. Frances, you're pale as a sheet and look weak'rn dish water." We'd all break in a run like young yearlings heading for the gate. In an effort to prove her wrong we'd start grabbing grub hoes and axes and head for the newground.

After proving our good health by making a pile of shrubs as large as a haystack we'd come bolting in to supper, never admitting we were the least bit tuckered out. But the work, 'the show', never helped. Mama'd already have her mind made up. Next trip Daddy made into town Mama'd send to the drugstore for the calomel pills.

Now Webster and I don't often disagree but I'm taking him to task this time. In his dictionary he defines calomel as a white, **tasteless** powder used as a cathartic. And he takes it even further and says it comes from the Greek root meaning, "beautiful, black." A misnomer if there has ever been one.

And I'm not the only one living who'll stand up and testify of the horribly bitter taste of the calomel used by our parents to "give us a good working out" every spring. Why just recently I polled fifty senior citizens, each privately, and their **very worst** childhood recollections were the tiny, pink pills they were required to take yearly. The calomel, if you please.

Actually the pink was a coating around the terrible calomel but seems most kids back then were like me; they had smaller esophaguses than folks do today. They just couldn't swallow those little pink pills but they had to keep trying and trying until long after the pink coating had dissolved and they were tasting the bitter - as - gall calomel.   A lady told me of having inadvertantly spit her pink pill into the water pail as she tried over and over to swallow it. I did worse than that.

Mama had coated my pill with corn bread to help me coax it down my throat. Long after the cornbread was swallowed, the awful pill remained. Eventually I choked, coughed, and the pill flew out — lost. Mama gave up and I was relieved and happy — until morning, that is.

I was still resting comfortably in my bed the following day when my Daddy arose, made the fire in the stove, put on the coffee, and proceeded to rinse his false teeth from their 'soaking cup' and place them in his mouth, as was his usual daily ritual.   It was then I, and the entire household, were awakened to his, "**Hell fire and damnation, Pearlie, what in the devil have**

you put in my teeth!" (And those adults who swallowed their little pink pills abruptly had never believed us when we tried to tell them they were bitter as gall. But even they, if any of them were still alive today — they would surely testify that taking one of those little boogers was tantamount to checking into the hospital and undergoing both an upper and a lower GI Series.)

I've just finished reading my newspaper. It says that scientific evidence has proven that some folks **do** get all down and out every year after Christmas. It says that it's the absence of lots of sunlight that causes folks to develop abnormalities in their brain chemicals. It causes your work to suffer, you to get the blues. In other words, to be listless, bilious, puny, green around the gills. In Mama's terminology, "to need a good spring tonic".

My Mama may be right. One thing for sure, we didn't spend much on doctor bills back then. Nor did we ever take a trip to Jamaica. So something our parents did for us must have been right.

Now I'm sure not recommending that you rush out and spend a lot of money foolishly, on little pink calomel pills that you can't swallow. Instead, send for another of my little books - it'll bring that needed sunlight into your life and do you as much good as a spring tonic; it will be a lot more pleasant!

Jessie James Introduced Me to the Wildflower World

There are six tiny little Bluets in a milk jug lid near my kitchen sink, the part of my morning walk that I could not resist bringing home. Throughout the day they snatch me from the pressures of a story deadline, reminding me of the peacefulness and beauty of the meadow in the early dew with its millions of tiny, two - inch - high blue flowers growing with only God's care.

Apart in a taller vase I also have other wildflowers: snips of the bright Yellow Jessamine vine which I carefully untangled from it's creeping over a small wateroak tree, primroses which wilted almost as soon as I picked them from the roadside, and a couple of the blue Buttonbush flowers whose stems cried profusely when I broke them. Among them are some yellow dandelions also, which, if I had left alone, would have become feathery white parachutes and blown free with the wind in a very few days. I love wildflowers; have loved them ever since Jessie James introduced me to them.

It was during WW II when my mother's sister, Aunt Jessie James, lived across the road from us for a couple of years. On Sunday afternoons in the springtime while her husband, Earl, and her boys, Bobby and Preston, joined by my Daddy and brother Bill - while the menfolk busied themselves trying to mend an inner tube and blow up a tire for Earl's old car, Jessie would walk out to visit with Mama.

It was a great treat for Mama, having Jessie nearby once more. And under the pretense of following a hen who had stolen her nest in the woods, the two would light out toward the trees, hollering back to my oldest sister Frances to keep an eye out for the babies. And I, maintaining a respectable distance least I be sent back also, would trail the two, knowing that they'd soon be passing back and forth some high - level 'womenfolk information.'

And sure enough, as soon as the two were into the pasture's edge — as soon as I, nonchalantly, had sauntered over and picked up some paw - paws left from the winter before and had started humming, "Picking up paw - paws puttin' 'em in your pocket" — as I began humming as if that were my sole mission I heard Aunt Jessie say, "Guess you heard that Fannie Mae is in the 'Family Way' again." "You don't say!" my Mama countered, flabbergasted, "Why heaven's forbid."

"Some say Jeb's insisting she git herself into town to see the doctor, what with the last two being born dead with only the midwife there."

"Pore, pore soul, when's she due?" Mama pursued the issue, trying to keep her voice down but forgetting that my young ears were within hearing.

Lady Luck had smiled on me. As an eleven - year - old I then had some juicy gossip that would get me into standing with the fifteen - year - old set when walking to church the next time. With that accomplished I heard Aunt Jessie yell, "Pearlie, just look't that patch of violets."

As they oooohed and aaaaaghed over them, "Never saw one bigger than that one," "Can you believe how deep that purple is! Just as velvety as velvet can be!" — carrying on over the wild flowers they seemed not to notice that I had joined them in picking a handful of the beauties.

Then together we three walked onward, deeper into the forest, me remaining silent lest my speaking make them aware of my intrusion on their rare time together. They pointed out the flurry of blackberry blooms that spring and hoped for lots of the fruit for jams and jellies.

Near some fallen logs Aunt Jessie spied the purplish little flowers and screamed, "Pearlie! Pearlie! Look't these Hepaticas, and, my sakes, there's some Trillium blooms! And is that a Bunchberry there? Pearlie remember when we were both working at the hospital and we got that Sunday off in the spring of — my, it musta been '28 — and remember that boy I was dating from up home, he came and got us from church, and a whole bunch of us young folks walked in the woods that spring afternoon. I believe these are the first Hepaticas I've seen since then. Many years ago. "I crept in quietly, surveying the beautiful blooms the two were exclaiming over, drinking deeply of their unspoiled beauty also.

Almost as if they forgot the time, forgot for once their ever - pressing domestic duties, the two — whom I deemed old women then as they neared their forties — forgetting their hard lives they became young again and walked onward, searching the forest's floor for more treasures. As they were rewarded in their pursuit, I shared in their treasures.

That afternoon my kin introduced me to the white flowers of the Wild Hydrangea. And to the Jack - in - the - Pulpit, a sort of green plant whose leaf curled out over a little stick - like minister who preached from his pulpit down there in the swamp. And to the May Apple which had a cup - shaped flower that hid beneath two large, umbrella - like leaves. And had little green sort of mock - apples on the plant; Aunt Jessie shared that she'd heard of some making jelly from them.

My Mama and her sister screamed like school girls once more when they saw the beautiful white flower of the Bloodroot. They pulled up a sprig to confirm that it was, indeed, the plant they'd known in their youth with the red root which they, and the Indians before them, had used as war paint.

They permitted me to pluck samples of the pink Lady's Slipper, the Pitcher Plant with it's cute little pitcher, and of the rare ghostly White Indian Pipe to take back to the house to show my siblings. It was an afternoon to remember! A day that had set my heart to humming for all time to come, humming over discovering the wild flowers that grow around me.

I learned to love and identify so many in the years that followed: the purple and the

Golden Asters, the Black - eyed Susans, the Morning Glories — there were white ones, pink ones, and tiny, tiny little blue ones. Daddy hated them growing around the corn in the field but I felt they were God's gift to make the work - day go better.

Even the old prickly thistles in the pasture had beautiful pinkish - purplish blooms. And the members of the cactus family which we sometimes encountered over at the gravel pit, the prickly pears, put forth a beautiful yellow flower not unlike a wild rose. And, aaahhh, the wild rose itself was something to behold. Mama once allowed one to grow in our yard's edge, alongside her tame Seven Sisters rose bush.

The sturdy red flower called a Trumpet Creeper was a fascination to me since we knew it as a Snake Flower; I always kept my distance, afraid it attracted snakes. But I failed, as a child, to appreciate the delicate Queen Anne's Lace since it's greenery was sticky, irritating to the skin.

Mama introduced us to Sweet Shrubs early in life; in fact, we most always had one of the trees growing in our yard. The good smelling blooms were plucked on Sunday mornings and wrapped into a handkerchief for taking to church. They were our perfume, the warmer the blooms grew as they were clutched in our hankies, the more fragrant they became.

We called the May Pop just that, while

some called it a Passion Flower. They and the little Sleepy Babies, called a Sensitive Briar by some, were two of the fringe benefits of a hot day's work in the cotton patch. The latter had little pink puff ball flowers and leaves that would curl up and *go to sleep* when touched.

Even the pesky Beggar - Lice had a pretty pink flower before it turned into little seeds that clung onto everything and everybody. Down through the years whenever I encountered wildflowers whose identify I didn't know I'd take them home for Mama's naming, or try to make it to Aunt Jessie's house; after all it was my own Jessie James who had first opened up to me the beautiful world of wildflowers.

Planting by the Signs: Peas in Every Pot

The world's population continues to increase: the need for producing more and better food weighs heavily on the farmer's heads. My Uncle Gray, an octogenarian, would quickly recommend "planting by the signs" as the best way for supply and demand to meet, albeit a controversial plan.

"You better not plant corn when the moon's a'fillin' out," my relative warns. "If'n you do the corn'll grow tall as the mischief. And the ear'll be jest 'bout as high as you can reach, 'n the little ole nubbins'll be 'bout like that," he says, indicating a four, five inch length of corn.

"But," he continues with advice that could put cornbread into the stomachs of all the world's hungry, "if'n you'll wait 'til after the full moon, when it's a sankin' (sinking, waning), the ears'll be 'bout hip high on the stalks, and sometimes they'll grow t' twenty inches long."

Another acquaintance of mine, a top - notch gardener who's also provided plenty of grub for folks in her day, concurs with my kin when it comes to relying on the signs. "Plant okra or beans when the signs're in the arm — and they'll bear — **Law, Law, They'll bear!** But don't eben think 'bout plantin' when the flow'rs in bloom — if'n you do, they'll just bloom, bloom, bloom, and you'll get no fruit a'tall," the serious Mrs. Sanford stresses.

Let's just suppose that the Federal Government would come out with a recommendation that farmers in America begin immediately to implement 'planting by the signs.' Think of the money we would save initially, not having to fund a major study, nor even subsidize a publication for reference. *The Farmer's Almanac*, in existence for two hundred years, would suffice completely.

Let's see, consulting the *Almanac* just now, page 8, it says: In April I should plant my "above ground crops" on either April 1, 2, 3, 8, 25, 26, 29 or 30. And my "root crops" can be put in on either of nine different days, unless of course I'm transplanting them. In which case, like my onion transplants, I can only put them out between April 24th and April 30th.

Seed beds 'can go' on April 1, 2, 3, 11, or 12 — or they're gonna hafta hold up a couple more weeks and get put in on April 29th or 30th. There's a catch, however, if the seed beds include flowers. The things of beauty are restricted to April 1, 2, 3, 8, 9, and 10. And, just to think, all these years when I've not gathered any zinnias for my kitchen table I thought it was because my husband kept cutting them down with the lawn mower. Now I realize the root cause for my failure to enjoy the beautiful blossoms lay with the fact that I had put them in on the wrong day.

Now I also know why my turnips never grew roots of any size either. If I had only listened to Cornelia Ann and Emmadel, the two spinisters who lived across the hill from us 'Up on Pea Ridge.' They knew, "Ye gotta git 'em in in the dark o' th' moon, if'n you wanna make any turnips, onions, beets, or 'taters." And, sure as shooting, every year they'd pile enough giant turnips in a hill to last them and the neighbors all winter long. Not to mention the sweet 'taters, and the beet pickles they'd have. And the scad of onions they'd hang from the ceilings; their root crop 'twas a right good start at feeding the world.

I heard recently of a Japanese researcher who claims that the key to increased yields and bigger beans lies in exposing the seeds to a strong magnetic field, say 10,000 times more magnitized that the earth's normal magnetic field. He and many others (some of whom I've met personally) will phoo - phoo the notion of planting by the signs. They'll affirm, then often contradict, like old Mr. Jergie, that, "I plant in the ground, and not in the signs. I alluz plant my cotton when th' ground's ready, gen'elly 'bout the 15th to the 18th uf April. And I do like 't git my beans and cucumbers in on Good Friday. And September 17th is the time t'sow yer fall turnips."

I remember the year we made a huge potato crop. Gathered and stored them only to have them all rot within a month. "Failed t' dig 'em on th' light uf the moon," friend Erton advised; somehow I believed him. Maybe it was because the apples he picked on the light of the moon every year kept longer than any others around. And because the time a tornado uprooted all the trees in the community except his, Erton explained, "My trees've got big, deep roots. I planted them years ago when the signs wuz in the feet; that way the roots've grown more than the tops have. If'n you plant 'em when 'th moon's a - growin' th' tops'll just grow 'n grow, more'n the roots."

One skeptic of sign planting recently related this story. Seems a farmer planned to plant his crop when the sign was right in May but it rained.

"Are you gonna go ahead and plant soon as it's dry?" his neighbor asked. "Not on your life," came the reply, "I'm waitin' 'til the signs are right in June." In June the rains fell again. "Planting now?" he was again asked. And the second time the reply came back, "No, waiting for the signs in July." "Well," the disgusted neighbor replied, "You can save both 'a plantin' and 'a gatherin,' too." (Since in July it would be too late for the crop to make.)

But here we are in a new decade with the ever increasing question: "How do we feed the masses?" You can decide which side of the camp you're on — exposing seeds to magnetic fields, or planting by the signs. As for me I've seen the handwriting on the wall and I'm lining up with the latter group. I've talked with too many old timers, my Uncle Gray included, who've testified of 50, 60, 70 years of planting and gathering by the signs who've always had peas in their pot.

Essie: One Sent to Warm Hearts

She couldn't read a book nor even write her name. She butchered the king's English; never held a job. In fact she was most fifty years old when a loving sister - in - law taught her to make her own bed. But as long as God gave her breath, Essie warmed hearts.

She was the child of Granny Melvina and Grandpa Bill's old age, one who never became other than a child. An Aunt or Great Aunt to more than three score folks, myself included; yet called that by none. To everyone she was just "Essie."

Those of us who knew Essie — both kith and kin — will not forget her now that her dear face has gone from us. For to know her was to love her, endlessly. It seems to us that inevitably new Webster books will list the word and definition: "ESSIE — warmer of hearts, a child - like one sent from God to show and receive love on earth."

Essie had an agelessness about her that endured; she was ever the same. Oh, those last few years found the near octogenarian struggling with diabetes and arthritis but still the same in spirit as when she was free on a fall day to sprightly take her bubbling bulk to the corncrib to shuck corn for the brother with whom she made her home.

Oh, on those bygone days Essie would mumble for the benefit of the nearby nieces and nephews; grumble under her breath as if she didn't enjoy the tasks that she did so well. But even while she hurried from the house toward the barn, saying, "I better commence shellin' a turn 'o corn 'fore Ferman Porter comes in home 'a rarin.'" Even while Essie said it there'd be a little smile creeping around the corners of her mouth. And we, like she, knew that she had nothing to ever fear from Ferman. His harshest words would be to quietly say, "Well, Baby, I thought you'uz gonna shell some corn fer me today."

Most of the time she'd take care of the corn shucking and the shelling punctually, having several turns ready by mill day. And see to it that the firewood was stacked neatly on the porch and that there was abundant stovewood piled behind the big Home Comfort out in the kitchen.

And during all of her labors she had to contend with aggravating nieces and nephews swarming underfoot; young'uns whose greatest joy in life was to upset Essie and get her to cussing. Get her to saying those four letter words whose use she was indulged but for which we would have our mouths washed out with soap. And for which Granny would bring her Bible and gently give us a little sermon on the saving grace of the Lord Jesus, and about not taking His name in vain.

One of my sisters admits to tying Essie's apron strings to a rocking chair years ago. Many of us have to ante up to being one of the cousins group who persisted in putting dirt in Essie's snuff box just to hear her rare, "H_ _ _! what've you'nes done to my snuff?" she'd demand, spitting and spurting just after pouring a big dip into her protruding lip. "D_ _ _ !D_ _ _! D_ _ _! I'm telling Granny Porter and yo Mama, Pearlie Maebell, on you!" she'd threaten, dipping the gourd dipper time and time again into the water bucket on the porch shelf, trying to get the dirt out of her mouth. Meanwhile we silly cousins were bent double, giggling like crazy over her amusing antics and her language.

Within a few minutes, however, we'd be heading for the shade tree with the straight chairs and the Stamps - Baxter song books. Essie with her childlike forgiveness would be happy again, excited because she loved to *have church*. And she'd sit there with her song book upside down *letting 'er rip*. "Amazing Grace" was her favorite. Then "Rock of Ages," "Leaning on the Everlasting Arms," "Bringing in the Sheaves."

Essie'd keep fanning with her funeral parlor fan and singing away, saying, "Let's us sang anuther'n, whatchasay Nonie Faye?" before we could catch our breaths from the previous one. And when we young'uns took time out to climb into the tree to better reach the ripe mulberries, Essie'd use the time for confession.

"Hey, Sis," she'd say, "You not gonna tell my preacher 'bout me saying that cuss word, are ye? I ain't gonna do it no more."

And sometimes we'd tease her further. "Essie, yo preacher would have a fit if he knowed you dipped snuff." Or "I bet yo preacher don' t know 'bout that pack 'o ready rolls you've been smoking."

"Sho nuff!" she'd be startled, "you won't tell him, will ye?" Always adding, "I ain't gonna do it no more."

Essie had recognized God's claim on her life and given her heart to Jesus at an early age. She was baptized into the Hannah Methodist Church near her home and maintained her loyalty to it for decades, until her death. If there was anything that excited her it was going to church. When a visitor came one of the first things Essie mentioned was her church. She'd say, "This Sunday is sanging at my church." Or, "Gertrude Hickman is a'making me a new dress to wear to th' Decorating at Hannah's, you know, fer the second Sunday in May."

If Essie had to miss a service she'd be mad as a hornet and report, "Aw, the devil, Ferman wadn't feeling no good and I didn't git to go to preaching."

She loved her preachers, too, and would often say, "I've gotta go to church a'Sunday and pay my preacher." She'd get out the preachers' pictures, saying, "Wanna see my feller? Now don'tcha tell nobody, ye hear?"

Essie cherished pictures in general, not just those of her preacher. When someone visited she'd ask,

"Got any pitchers, Nellie Sue?"

"Here. These are my grandkids. This is Carmen's little girl," Sue would answer, producing pictures.

"Aw, the douse, it ain't donnit," Essie'd

protest, followed in the same breath with, "Oh, God, ain't 'er purty. Gertrude, come 'ere and see 'er."

Next to inquiries about photos from visitors Essie's second most asked question was , "Got any chewing gum, Sis?" And the excitement and appreciation the simple minded girl exhibited encouraged folks to never come without bringing her a package of Juicyfruit or Spearmint. It was always an exchange that warmed others' hearts even more than it did Essie's.

When Essie occasionally rode into town on Saturday afternoon with Gertrude and Ferman she asked for nothing more than to talk with folks, warming the hearts of both friends and strangers. And before they left for home again she'd say, "Ferman, I reckon I wanta drank a sodie water" (soft drink).

Essie had a thing for names. She called those closest, her dear caregivers — Aunt Gertrude who cared for her more than four decades, and Geraldine, the niece who sacrificed for her the last two years she was on earth — these she'd call "Gert," "Pet Box," or even "Mama."

The child - lady born Essie Gaberela Porter seldom referred to anyone with a single name, calling dear neighbors, "Mack Fair" and "Vonie Pearson." She'd call her nieces, "Brenda Inez," "Trillie Murbell" (never just Trillie),   "Mury

'Luzbeth" (not Elizabeth) and "Sair Mell" (not Sara) like others did.

Regardless of what Essie called us, we were thankful that she knew us. But most of all we'd like to say, "Thank you God for letting *us* know Essie. For permitting her to come and live among us to bring laughter to our lives and warmth to our hearts."

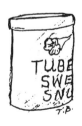

It's Barefoot Time Again

With Good Friday behind us and the Whippoorwills' calls drawing nigh my feet are again itching to be set free. It's as if they know that shoes are a bondage imposed by society, not God. Well, when Adam and Eve hid their nakedness with fig leaves they didn't need shoes to come before God, did they?

Actually, it is only recently that social rules have dictated the wearing of these restricting contrivances upon one's feet during all waking hours. It was not so when I was growing up during the Great Depression. Back then it was unheard of that after the passing of the cold months a strapping young boy — or girl either, for that matter — would purchase a pair of new shoes for honing his running skills. Those who won foot races in my day did it barefoot. Being able to dig their toes into the sand at the starting line gave them an edge.

To be truthful, it was unusual that kids got new shoes of any kind in warm weather. As soon as Daddy started turning the soil shoes were cast aside. No foot massager invented by man will ever equal the soothing comfort afforded my *tootsies* as I, early each spring, plunged them into the freshly plowed sand.

This often meant slipping around behind Mama's back for a week or two — being the stickler she was, insisting that "barefoot time comes **after** the first whippoorwill's call." One year, desperate to release our feet, Bill and I even talked Daddy into helping our cause. At dusky - dark one evening he fooled Mama with his mock "whip - whip - whip - poor - will" call from out behind the barn.

Regardless of the means by which I came about that first barefoot time of the season, it was heaven to be rid of my ill - fitting - oxfords and holey socks. To swap in my hand - me - down clod hoppers for the cold earth squashing through my hungry toes. After a few days in the soft soil, with its occasional snags and rocks, my feet began to get toughened. Before summer's end I was able to almost keep pace with my brother Bill as we raced barefoot down the gravel road. And I was only too happy that going without shoes was stylish back then. It was stylish for everything but church - going twice weekly, and the very youngest got by with even that.

But back to our purchasing footgear come warm weather. During those lean years Daddy would, of necessity, get a pair of cheap brogans in the spring to plow in. These would either be ordered from the cattylog or put on our 'ticket' at the mercantile where they were 'advancing us' until cotton selling time. More often than not the new rough leather shoes would rub such huge blisters on Daddy's feet until he'd threaten to make slits in them or to cut out small holes for his toes like he had done in his old pair.

Mama never was one for going barefoot. Yet being the unselfish one she was, she'd never mention getting new footwear for herself. Instead she'd insist that Daddy's decade - past church shoes in their worn - out - and - tied - together - with - strings state — that the cast off shoes "suit me just fine for the field and barn and house."

Most of us kids made - do with hand - me - downs from each other, or neighbors, or cousins for the short hours on summer Sundays. At those times our feet required shoes two sizes larger than in winter; it took the extra to compensate for the spreading - out our feet did from going barefoot.

Mama also helped stretch the shoe budget by refastening floppy shoe soles with glue or screen tacks. And she often pushed her huge rug-hooking needle in and out to resew ripped shoe uppers. Once Mama had a bad accident while mending heavy cotton sacks with that same multi

- duty rug needle.   The huge needle's eye, threaded with twine raveled from guano sacks — well, the needle's blunt end penetrated the thimble and plunged backward underneath Mama's fingernail.

Bracing herself against the pain and the inclination to faint, Mama bit down on her lip and pulled the needle out — and hardly slacked up on the exacting chore she was performing for her family.

Shoe dyes were also used extensively by my Mama to lengthen the life of terrible looking shoes during those Depression days.   And if someone **did chance** to get white shoes in spring then the shoes certainly **had** to be dyed black or brown come September, making them presentable for wearing in the fall and winter. Back then it was more socially accepted to be seen barefoot than to be caught wearing white shoes past September first.

When we awoke on Sunday mornings and there was no black polish to ready Daddy's dark shoes for church attendance another make - do came into play.   They were rubbed with a cold, left - over biscuit; the lard in the bread did the 'shining' trick, I believe.

The one *frivolity* in spring shoe buying was for my sister Frances.   When she began courtin' it was absolutely necessary that she get a pair of white heels from the Sears, Roebuck Cattylog.

The cheapest pair available was, ironically, the one she usually *liked best*.

After Mama sold off roosters to the rolling store for the money, Frances' foot had to be measured before mailing the shoe order. This was done by my oldest sibling standing on a piece of tablet paper while Mama drew little lines in front of her big toes, on either side of her toes, and behind her heel.

Then before many days the beautiful shoes would arrive with the letter carrier. To take better care of her treasure Frances often toted them most of the way to and from church. She put the shoes on and off within sight of the edifice; that prevented the gravel's tearing at the new white leather of the shoes.

Yes, springtime back then was a blessing, financially speaking, since it saved on buying shoe leather. And I was only too glad to cast aside my outgrown patched shoes for toe freedom in the dirt.

Reebok commercials today tell us to do our own thing in relation to shoes. **But** society keeps talking differently — signs on doors where folks gather to sop biscuits and gravy often indicate "no bare feet."

And recently I read where a lawyer — who probably had bunions like my Daddy did from having to wear old cheap shoes — well, seems this hard - up lawyer wore his old green tennis shoes while presenting a case in court.

Guess that judge had never been *pore* himself cause he up and sentenced that lawyer to a week in jail for making out with what he had — and for having his feet comfortable to boot. I don't know what this world's a - comin' to but one thing I do know. With springtime upon us and my feet a'itchin,' I favor getting back to basics like God intended and letting folks bare their feet whenever they get a'hankerin.'

Line Up Here to Pick the Tater Bugs

On a hot spring day a battalion of huge red wasps besieged me in the attic. Without hesitation I passed up the opportunity to do as my Daddy'd have done in the 30s — to roll up a Country Gentleman magazine and "fly into 'em, hoping for the best." A can of *Hot Shot Wasp Killer* is what saved my hide, **and** prevented a hospital visit over my allergy to wasp stings.

I see the predicament I faced that day as paralleling, in some ways, that of today's farmers. They are being harassed by environmentalists for their use of pesticides and insecticides. Now I'm concerned about our environment, too. Why, I'm hopping mad at this very writing about the foolish environmental destruction being wrought on my neighborhood, my county, by the methane gas drillers. But recently given a choice in my fight with the fierce insects in my attic, I opted for the more sensible solution, albeit an environmentally questionable one.

Farmers today also have an alternative when it comes to using or not using chemicals to destroy harmful insects. My Mama knew about, but had no choice but to practice, the 'without chemicals route' years ago. And I'd like to see those who're having the biggest conniption fits about today's use of insecticides — I'd like to see them have to produce our nation's food supply while my Mama supervised their 'tater bug pickin.'

I can envision it now — the thousands of sign - toting city slickers throwing down their 'HALT THE USE OF INSECTICIDES' placards and lining up for fruit jars with kerosene in them. And Mama there, giving the novices instructions about fanning out across the acres and acres of irish 'taters.

I can hear her instructing on the necessity of gently turning every single leaf on every solitary 'tater plant to pick off the destructive bugs. And how they should be especially careful to look inside the still - tightly - curled leaves, for lurking there they'd likely find scads of fat baby bugs. "Sometimes," Mama'd say, "you can just press the sides of the leaves together and squish the hundreds of unhatched yellow eggs, or the miniature newborns with their smooth brown skin — just kill off hundreds with one squish."

Just thinking of it I can picture those protestors turning bilious green, especially when their jars start filling up with the creepy, crawly things. And they'll probably be worse'n my sister, Trillie. Here's the story:

Once when we were out of kerosene Mama told us to pick our jars full of the pests which were eating our potato plants to the nub — to pick them, and later kill them on a big, flat rock at the end of the 'tater patch. Well, my baby sister was real squeamish, couldn't handle it. When no one was looking she buried her pint of bugs in the freshly - turned soil, thinking to smother 'em to death.

'Course Mama came along 'bout the time the grown bugs with their speckled hard shells were escaping, unscathed, from the earth. Mama made my Sis "lick her calf over." Until this day I can hear my sibling yelling and see her shivering, hating the crushing of those bugs. And till this day she hates worms and bugs, almost lets it halt her love of fishing.

But Trillie's repulsion long ago was minor compared to what we're gonna see soon outta those 'tater - bug - toting town folks, especially if the fields are so wet they'll mire a buzzard's shadow, and if the workers have to get barefoot and let the mud squish between their toes as they pick.

And I bet you they'll be afeared fer their lives when Mama starts 'em in on gettin' those huge worms offen the tomato plants. It'll take those new pickers awhile for their eyes to get adjusted so's they can see the long, fat green creeps which have antennas sticking outta their heads.

And, oooowheeeee—just think 'uh when they have to smash those big tomato-plant-cutting camouflaged creatures! What with those anti - poison folks never having seen a green worm curled inside a half - eaten tomato, thanks to the farmers and the insecticides, what with them being so unfamiliar with worms and how they squirt when smuushed—they'll probably be looking like a bunch of green snuff - dippers in no time flat.

And I predict it'll get worse 'n worse as they have to pick the worms off the cabbages and the collards and when they have to dig down into the ground beside the little fallen bean plants, trying to dig out and crucify the cutworms responsible for the destruction. Yep, it's gonna be rough on those protestors - turned farmers as they frantically try to provide green vegetables for this entire nations' anti - cholesterol diets. I can imagine that it won't be long until they'll start to

believe that pests do actually destroy 30% or about $20 billion worth of crops in the U.S. every year — even when the farmers are using pesticides. And they'll soon be wanting to kiss the feet of the man who invented DDT, like I did back in the late 40s.

Picking up punctured boll weevil squares till their backs break will make the dissenters happy to see black strap molasses, arsenic, and water being mixed and applied to cotton plants to kill the boll weevils — like we rejoiced in the 40s. This is not to mention how they'll begin praising the efforts of today's farmers at controlling boll weevils with boll weevil perfume and sterile boll weevils.

And if they were shot backward in a time capsule to 1926 when, according to my 85-year-old Uncle Ferman, the cotton crop was **completely, down to the last boll, destroyed** by the boll weevils — well, if today's anti - pollution organizers had to try to clothe folks in cotton under such circumstances they'd lighten up on their criticism of man - made pesticides, I do believe.

Waking up from an operation in a hospital bed that was covered with chinches or discovering the gruesome, biting bed bugs all over your motel room as two ladies shared with me they did in the 30s — these experiences will shed new light on the use of pesticides also.

Or contacting head lice at school can enlighten one. Having to shampoo nightly with some ghastly - smelling treatment and then comb your head for hours on end with a sharp, fine - toothed comb in an effort to get the lice eggs out of your hair. Going through this ordeal, hoping to end the awful cycle of head lice, like so many of us did years ago, will make one think twice about banning pesticides.

Having weevils ruin the corn in the crib and the dried peas in the loft that are your main food for the cold winter ahead. Or having to contend with house flies in the hot days when window screens were a scarcity. When, if company came to take dinner with you, all hands were enlisted and given guano sacks to 'herd' the flies out the back door. And then a green peach tree bough was kept handy to chase any intruding flies from the vicinity of the table while you ate. This latter experience will make one thrilled to be able to purchase a small metal fly - sprayer and fill it with one cup of *Watkins' Fly Spray*; make one excited to have a chemical that will kill off the pesky and dirty insects.

Biting into apples and finding half a worm, spending all day trying to get plant lice off the mess of turnip greens before cooking them for supper, having cabbage worms destroy your chances for winter kraut — these things will make you grateful for scientists who've invented pesticides and for farmers who now use them, make you thankful for the great progress the farmers are making, even down to using computer software, *Chemrank* and *Fairs*, to help with proper pesticide applications.

Oh, I'd be the first one to say, "Get rid of all chemicals" — if it'd work. My Daddy was so careful when he rinsed that arsenic - dripping pan, wouldn't allow it within half - a - mile of the spring or the well. Knew it was dangerous but that it was the only thing that'd allow us to make half a cotton crop.

And we tried making out with just nature in the garden. Petted and pampered those lady bugs, trying to keep them so they'd expel unwanted insects. And we planted the stinking marigold flowers in the garden to chase off bad bugs. And tossed hot sand into the corn's tassels, trying to kill the corn borers without chemicals. Nurtured our soil with just the proper amount of chicken and cow manure; added compost made from rotted fruit and vegetable matter. But it would only do so much. As a result we could barely grow enough food to feed our own family, with two adults and nine kids working around the clock, around the year.

But that sad tale isn't true with today's agriculture thanks to the availability of chemicals. My hat's off to today's farmers — more food and better than ever before, with fewer and fewer folks required to do the job. So I say — the very next time these off - base environmentalists start getting hot under the collar and throwing off on farmers — I say — let's just mail out application forms which specify: **"SIGN HERE TO PROTEST THE USE OF CHEMICALS BY FARMERS — AND TO VOLUNTEER TO BE THE FIRST IN LINE TO PICK THE 'TATER BUGS!"**

Old Maude And I Are Skeered Uf Bridges
(AND BILL'S TROLL'S TO BLAME FOR OUR BRIDGEOPHOBIA)

A friend invited me down for the day. Although I longed to go I concocted all sorts of excuses. The real reason I wouldn't go, however, is because her house is accessible only by crossing a sky - high, narrow bridge. The bridge scares me nigh to death, causes me to clinch my steering wheel until my hands become rigid, my heart to palpitate wildly; bordering on a heart attack.

It's the same panic that for years limited my visits to my own dear mother; we lived on opposite sides of a river over which there was only a lift bridge.   The low hanging structure would at times have its midsection raised to permit river traffic to flow through.   And whenever I was caught, detained, on the bridge during this procedure I thought "pass over Jordan, I will for sure."

In Europe on an extended honeymoon I encouraged my hubby to "Go on ahead, tour Ludwig's castle without me."   The gleaming white edifice in Southern Germany could be reached only by walking across a swinging, swaying bridge suspended hundreds of feet above the mother of all gullies.   It was not too far advanced, in my way of thinking, beyond the tangled vines used by cave men when swinging across ravines. And God had in these advanced days blessed me with a higher level of intelligence, one with sense enough to avoid such death - traps.

And there was the time when my youngest sister, Trillie, and I set out on a motor trip , taking along our combination of four little offsprings and our Mama. If I had know when I approached that bridge abutment down near New Orleans, Louisiana that I was getting onto the world's longest bridge, the Lake Pontchartrain Causeway extending approximately 29 miles — ! Let's just say it was a miracle that I reached the other side — what with my eyes squinched tightly, my hands a' tremblin'.like the Saint Vitus Dance, and my heart bursting out of my chest.

My mind even calls up an instance when I was sitting in the rumble seat of an old Ford. Riding along on a lovely fall day at dusky dark I was feeling so rich and so secure, snuggled between my two older siblings and my dear Daddy who was holding onto his trusty 12-gauge shotgun. There we were motoring somewhere between Moore's Bridge and Echola, on our way to Grandma Shirley's to eat a wedding feast of roasted duck with Mama's only brother, Victor, and his new bride, Amy.

And my Daddy's brother Ferman, who had so graciously agreed to drive us over there for the occasion, and my Mama and the three smaller kids were riding in the front seat, all purring along at the unbelievable speed of about fifteen miles an hour. Happiness beyond measure until I saw the gigantic overhead metal beams of an old truss bridge looming in front of us. Daddy's explanation, "The famous Shirley Bridge," did nothing to relay the fear that swirled in my being with the same intensity the flood waters raged beneath the bridge that night.

No, this fear of crossing a bridge is not a new thing with me. In fact it goes back to when I was little more than a toddler. But it was only while working on a Master's Degree in Counseling that I read some from Sigmund Freud, the founder of psychoanalysis, and was able to put my finger on my brother Bill as the one who caused my fear of bridges, my bridgeophobia, if you please.

You see this feller Freud, (with whom I often disagree cause he don't leave much room for my God and my Jesus) — well, he talks about phobias. He says that this thing of having an intense, unreal fear of something goes back to my childhood. According to him, the thing feared is just like Mama putting a scarecrow out in her garden to make the crows think it is actually her out there all day long. That the thing I'm afeered of, bridges, is really just a symbol. A cover - up for some other fear. And the other fear comes from an event that occurred in my early childhood, something I've been repressing, hiding, keeping a lid on all these years. Or so Freud says.

Now it has finally all come to me, all become clear! I was only four but I could cross the big flat foot log from Granny's over to Timmons place. Just jump on the thing and whiz across it without looking downward; not a worry in the world about falling into the deep ditch.

Then one Sunday when I was walking the three mile roundtrip to the Hannah Methodist Sunday School — anxious to get those little lesson cards Mrs. Ward Fair gave me — well it was just me and Bill making the trip one Sunday. And right after we left our yard he commenced to tell me a tale about The Three Billy Goats Gruff and the terrible Troll who lived underneath the bridge. By the time we had walked the half - mile down to the sturdy wooden bridge (built over the creek by the WPA) — well, by the time we got there Bill had me scared nearly to death, afraid that vicious Troll was gonna jump from beneath the bridge timbers and holler, "Get off my bridge" and worried that before I could do it the horrid creature that Bill described would come running, shouting, his red eyes blazing, heading straight in my direction.

So in order to ensure my passage that day I got down on all - fours and looked underneath the bridge. And while Bill fussed and fumed that we were going to be late for church and that I was getting mighty dirty — well, I crawled all the way across the bridge. I stopped to check at every crack between every board, making sure the troll was nowhere in sight.

I felt a little better when Good Brother Manderson prayed the benediction that morning, asking God to "give everybody a safe trip home." But I just couldn't quite get shed of the fear of that troll. So en route home I again crawled across the bridge, this time afraid that I might fall through one of the cracks and be eaten by the monster. To make matters worse, Bill sneaked up close behind me and hollered, "I'm coming up to eat you!" I screamed and ran the final half - mile home.

After that day I was afraid to cross the foot log over to Timmons, or the slimy, moss - covered one that we had to take when we went over to see Aunt Beck and Uncle John Hannah. I almost quit going to Sunday School because I was so afraid of the bridge down below our house.

And in later years I became afraid to cross tall bridges, short bridges, wooden bridges, cement bridges. I thought I had developed an unnatural fear or phobia of the slippery log, and a fear of falling through the wide cracks on old wooden bridges and a fear of falling into the swirling water — since I can't swim. And though the years I thought Daddy had to get out of the wagon and lead the mules across bridges because they were, especially Old Maude, and particularly when they weren't wearing their blinders — because they were, like me — jittery of the cracks or the water underneath the bridges.

But no. Freud has helped me to see the light. I wasn't really afraid of the slippery log nor the bridges with cracks. Nor am I now afraid of the tall bridges, the long bridges, the old bridges. It is the troll that I fear, it has always been the fear of the troll that has kept me from visiting my Mama, my friend, from viewing the beautiful castle. It is fear that the troll is down in the water, under the bridges, in the gullies — fear of the troll that has kept me uptight ever since Bill told me about him when I was four.

Just think how much money a fear of the troll cost folks long years ago, what with them having to put sides on covered bridges to keep the mules from spooking. And just because Bill and the likes of him told folks and mules about the awful trolls living under the bridges.

So I'm sitting here waiting for the phone to ring again. If my friend who lives beyond the sky-high, narrow bridge calls with another invitation to visit, I am off without a second thought of that dangerous - looking structure.

I'm stopping at the stockyard, however, and buying the biggest goat with the longest horns that they have for sale. Then just let that mean old troll show his head around those bridge timbers. I can just hear that egotistical creature hollering, "Who's that tromping on my bridge? I'm coming up to eat you." And then my big goat replying, "I am the big Billy Goat Gruff. Come ahead." With one big butt my goat'll knock him into the water! That will be the end of the awful, threatening troll! And the end of Bridgeophobia for me and Old Maude. Then the only unfinished business I'll have will be with my big brother Bill.

Saddle Up And Ride
For Th' Doc

I'm summoning all my willpower, stamina, and optimism trying to convince myself I'm going to live past this episode the doctors have dubbed "an upper respiratory infection." And I'm consulting with my banker, my lawyer, and the loan sharks — trying to work out a way to pay the doctors and the druggists for their advice and remedies. It sets my melancholy heart to remembering good ole Doctor Shackleford, the country doctor who'd charge you $2.00 for a house call and throw in the medicine to boot.

My first acquaintance with the good
'Doctor Shack' was the night I was born. Now I
know they say that first impressions are the most
lasting but it wasn't so in this case. You see, my
Mama sort of influenced me **against** the fellow
on the night in question. There she was,
spending her first night in her new home — and I
decided to be born. And Doctor Shack had been
summoned to attend her.

Actually my Granny Porter had been in
town that day, bumped into the Doc, and told
him, "Pearlie's time's near, you oughtta drop by
tonight." Well, the doctor sat there by the
fireplace spitting chewing tobacco into Mama's
spic and span, brand new fireplace. And Mama
was peeved. Peeved over the tobacco juice and
peeved that the doctor just seemed to sit there,
doing nothing, while her pains grew worse and
worse. But eventually he gave her — my
teetotaling Mama — a little toddy, I believe the
story goes. Many times, however, country doctors
could do little more than "bide their time" while
attending the sick.

Whereas Doctor Shack did have a T -
Model to drive the few miles to our house the
night of my birth, in the earlier days of his
practice he, and his fellow practitioners, traveled
by horseback or by buggy. They carried their
expertise in their heads, their equipment and
medicine in little black bags, and big doses of love

and devotion for the people in their hearts. And many times during the Great Depression their pay was paltry, and delayed, as was Doctor Shack's that February night after I was born. As he told Daddy, "Yer wife and baby's fine; I'll be heading home now," Daddy replied, "I'll just have to settle up later with ye, Doc, come gatherin' time."

Many a'time when a woman's delivery was spasmodic — her pains a'comin' and a'goin' — many a'time the good doctor would just let his team rest in the barn and he'd 'go to bed' in the patient's home. And then over into the wee hours of the morning, if the time came, he'd be handy for the delivery. And after the newborn was checked out and the mother given strict orders not to leave her bed for two weeks, the doctor'd leave for home. Sometimes he'd have a couple of bushels of sweet potatoes in the back of his wagon. Or a basket of apples, peaches, or several buckets of syrup if the farmer'd just completed his syrup making. And occasionally he'd have five dollars in his pocket.

A friend of mine, Kathleen, was deemed worth "half - a - ham" by her Papa. Or at least the doctor was paid one entire ham for delivering her twin brother and her. Another acquaintance's entry into the world was finalized by dropping a few bales of pea - vine hay off at the doctor's barn (pea - vine hay being the worst sort of hay imaginable, you understand). And my dear preacher friend, Brother Ed King, says his father "plunked down twenty - five dollars because he was so happy to have a boy after having two girls."

I'm not sure just how modern physicians set their fees, maybe by the Dow Jones. But some doctors long ago, reportedly, set their fees for house calls at the going rate for postage stamps. Stamps were two cents so house calls were two dollars; office visits one dollar. And even then, the one, two dollars were paid in chickens, eggs, milk, butter.

Doctoring must have, at times, seemed like an unthankworthy calling. Heard of one dedicated doctor who, along with his nurse wife, drove miles into a mountainous area, then parked their car and hiked to the poor cabin. They labored all night saving a woman and her child from what seemed almost certain death. Their reward came only from God; the husband not only failed to compensate them, he sneaked out while they labored and stole the gas out of their car.

Country doctors long ago had to be resourceful. Dr. Wright of Berry, Alabama and his nurse wife set up a clinic during summers and took out tonsils by the scores, in an effort to relieve suffering by many children. We drove my sister Frances down in a wagon for the operation, hopeful it would help her hearing problem. After the surgery she was moved across the street from the good doctor's home to my Aunt Margaret's house. Two, three days later she was able to make the trip home in my Uncle Doc's log truck.

My husband tells of a similar clinic in his hometown of Moundville, Alabama long ago. Seems a doctor set up a hospital in the school one summer and removed tonsils coming and going. The bills for some of them are probably still outstanding, with interest.

Consider the case of the unusual father; he determined to pay the doctor a'plenty for his daughter's appendectomy. Someone described the procession into town as follows: The doctor in front with the sick girl in his Model - A - Ford, one son following the doctor with a wagon load of corn, another son coming behind the wagon, leading a milk cow, and the third son bringing up the rear, driving a sow with a rope around her hind leg.

A druggist in Mississippi confessed to me recently that as a son of a country doctor he missed his childhood; spent all of it stacking firewood and stovewood that was hauled to their house and dumped out — pay for his daddy's services to the area's sick. Yep, Doctor Shackleford and I got off on a bad foot but we soon patched things up. And I learned that he and other country doctors with whom I came in contact during my childhood were wondrous folk.

They not only were willing to come at the least notice — but they were willing to give their all — often knowing they'd not be paid for it.

They were willing to deliver a family's baby and — when the other kids ambled in from school — give an eye exam to the six year - old, check the ears of the nine - year - old, and advise the daddy about his high blood. They'd inquire as to how the teenage son's foot progressed after the rusty nail almost caused lockjaw last summer. Even wait for Jeff to come in from the barn and take off his shoe and check the foot.

Then maybe they'd encourage the teenage daughter to walk alone to the car with them and give her some 'teenage talk'; the doctors were terrific psychologists. And when they'd done their very best and it wasn't enough, they'd share their faith in the Almighty and help the brokenhearted to say, "The Lord giveth and the Lord taketh away. Blessed be the Name of the Lord."

Here I am — summoning my willpower, stamina, and optimism trying to live past this current infection. And wearing my phone book and my car tires thin — running from one physician to another, as I get the run - around with specialists trying to decide which strain of a virus I might have and whose category it falls under. My banker and my insurance company are busy giving me forms to sign — and I'm sitting here, wishing, longing for the Ole Days when Daddy'd saddle up and ride for the good ole country Doc.

Courtin' Jest Ain't What It Us'ta Be

I noted the certifieds in a paper recently; filled with advertisements by folks on the lookout for a date, a sweetheart, a mate, if you please. It made my mind turn backward; I started singing, like we did in school long ago:

"Oh, Miss, I'll give you a paper of pins,
If that's the way true love begins,
And I will marry you, you, you,
And I will marry you."

In the old folk song the boy offers the girl not only the paper of pins, but the key to his heart; she rejects both. He then extends the key to his chest so that she can have money at any request. She quickly agrees to the latter only to have him, laughingly, withdraw the offer, saying :

> "Ha, ha, ha, money is all,
> Ladies' love is nothing at all,
> And I'll not marry you, you, you,
> And I'll not marry you."

The fellow in the old ballad was going to have to pay big bucks to get his wife, his love. In a sense it's become that way today; the rage of the hour is computerized dating/matchmaking services whereby folks get their heartthrobs after paying out huge sums of money. It wasn't that way when I was comin' along. Come to think of it, however, young men were willing to sacrifice much more than money for future wives during my upbringing.

Buna tells of two young boys who, being more privileged than others their age, drove over in an old Ford about 4:30 one hot June day. Buna's two courtin' - age - daughters peered anxiously toward the yard as they kept hoeing away alongside their parents out in the cotton patch. D'rectly the visiting boys spied the folks and walked out into the field, the hot dusty sand covering the shoes they had recently polished.

After making their howdy - dos the boys up and asked if the girls could go to town with 'em, to see the pitch'r show. The girls, blushing over being caught in the field barefooted, with their bonnets on, were hoping with all their might they'd be permitted to go.

Their dad, the ultimate authority, didn't beat around the bush about it. "Ain't no need to ast' jest now. With this cotton patch grassed over the way it 'tis, they've gotta hoe til sundown and THEN git the cows up and do the milkin.' I reckin atter that they can go with ye, previded they don't lay out too late."

"How's about it if we do the hoeing for 'em?" the excited boys quickly volunteered. "Alright by me," Mr. Rowland drawled as the strong boys grabbed the hoes and the girls took off to call the cows up early and draw water out of the well for baths. Later as the four headed into town it was the boys (who'd been willing to do hard labor for their loves) who were hot and dusty, but happy nevertheless.

Belle tells a similar true tale. A young man once walked several miles to her home on the edge of a small town. He, too, had the picture show on his mind but Belle's guardian, her grandfather, had more pressing plans for her. The large pile of stovewood she was transferring from the woodpile to the dry underhouse area was on his mind. "The wood's gotta be moved b'fore ye go anywhere," Belle's grandpa was emphatic. The spruced up feller flew in; in no time a'tall the work was completed and Belle was permitted to walk with him to see a "Talkie." Considering the long walk he had back to his home after the date and the hard day he had waiting in the fields the following day makes me conclude the boy's "head must have really been turned" by that beautiful brunette, Belle.

Bro. Benny, now in his late 80s, says there was no getting around that walking, but he wouldn't have changed it. When he was only seventeen he walked about ten miles to see a sweet sixteen - year - old. Together they walked another five miles to a Brush Arbor meeting; the roundtrip entailed a walk of thirty miles for the strapping youth. "Well worth it," he now says. "Got to hold her hand for ten miles. **Well worth it!**"

Myrtis remembers long - ago next - door neighbor boys who maybe had a crush on her and her sister Ollie. Or perhaps it was just the thought of getting candy to eat during the days of sugar rationing during WW II that made the youths willing to slave for the girls. Nevertheless, the boys, Willie and Sam, knowing full well that the two girls would be doing their Saturday afternoon chore of scrubbing the kitchen's wooden floor always showed up at their house just after Saturday dinner. And invariably lazy Ollie would say, "I'd make some fudge if we didn't have to scrub this floor." "Immediately the boys would grab brooms and homemade rag mops and scrub that floor 'til it shined," Myrtis recently related. Then she added, "Soon a fire would be roaring in the wood stove, drying the floor and getting ready for the fudge to be made and shared among the four of us."

Yep, would - be suitors put up with lots in order to win the hand of maidens in days gone by; it was much harder than putting a little gas in a Mustang that Daddy is paying for and then treating the girl to a movie and pizza with cash from Mama, like youths do nowadays. In addition to the hard work they sometimes encountered, boys once had to reckon with fathers who held to unyielding principles. There were once men who wouldn't hear of their daughters going to the movies, especially not unless another sibling accompanied them on their outing. Many girls, and some boys, could not play cards; some fathers permitted the playing of Rook, but turned thumbs down on Bridge, associating that with gambling. Wouldn't let a girl go to a dance, but permitted things like tacky parties, going on 'possum hunts, or getting together to roast marshmallows or wieners down in the pasture, provided someone could scrap up the money for the wieners. I recall being surprised that I was permitted to attend an Easter egg hunt at night when I was about 16; boys brought lanterns for them and their sweeties to use for hunting the eggs which had been hidden earlier in the woods' edge.   Only the outstanding reputation of the sponsoring family made it possible for me to go. There were many times when my feller had to content with my daddy's "NO."

Today's matchmaking computers may be able to pair folks up but I'll have to live a long time before I'll believe they can do a better job of it than the "hands on experience" that convinced Kirk fifty years ago that Mary Nell would make a fine wife. Kirk helped Mary Nell's daddy with the plowing, planted the corn crop just to be near his heartthrob at the noon hour, I believe the story goes. And to get some of her good cooking, her homemade blackberry cobbler pie. Then seeing the feather bed and 'pillers' she had made after saving the soft chicken feathers for years and seeing her beautiful handiwork on homemade quilts and counterpanes was all it took to "do him in." Kirk would gladly have helped put in three or four corn crops to be near Mary Nell until they could be wed. He didn't want to risk anyone else beating his time (stealing his girl). He, like many other young men of my day and earlier, felt no sacrifice of hard work was too much for his true love. But times have changed; I haven't seen any boys plowing for someone's hand in marriage in a coon's age. When you come right down to it, courtin' jest ain't what it us'ta be!

I'm Keeping My Walls
Bare, Thank You
They Look Great Without
The Newspaper Pages

My friends constantly taunt me about my bare walls. Meanwhile they continue to hang things onto theirs. A three - foot wooden spoon, a bent coal shovel, and a straw broom worn to the nub all find themselves dangling near their fireplaces. There are groupings upon groupings of baskets — round baskets, square baskets, oval baskets, rectangular baskets — all clinging to tiny nails, catching dust.

Most everything that belonged to my friends' grannies has found itself upon their walls. Their specs in frames, the handkerchiefs that they took to church in frames, their doilies, the quilt pieces that they made for samples, and on and on my friends hang.

Some of them are into ducks, and chickens. They have stuffed chickens in half - baskets filled with straw, mid - way to their ceilings. Appliqued ducks, cross - stitched ducks, and ducks printed upon fabric and pressed into round crochet frames are there. The list of things that my friends hang on their walls ends only when every conceivable inch of wall space is covered.

Don't get me wrong. My friends mean well when they tease me about my empty walls, saying, "We **would** give Faye a picture for her wall but she doesn't have space enough to hang it." And I have to admit that their homes do look lovely. And that often I wish mine looked as well.

Now I do have a few things on my walls. I have one picture hanging, centered, over each table that sits directly against a wall. Period. It's the way my high school Home Economics teacher said I should have it. She warned us back then about hanging things out in the middle of space with no furniture underneath them. Not that I would have needed her warning, however. My aversion to things covering my wall is more deep - seated than high school.

I suppose my mind began to congeal on how a wall **should not** look when I was but a toddler playing on a pallet in the front room of a tenant house. As I lay there on a folded quilt beside my Mama's humming sewing machine — playing with my empty thread spools — I believe I realized at that moment that my world was amiss.

I think the breakthrough came as I stared at the old plank walls, darkened through the years by smoke that filled the rooms when folks tried to burn green pine logs in the fireplace. Or when they used too much kindlin' and great clouds of black smoke belched out, filling the place. I also think my childish mind began to shrink back, about that time, at the ugly scars on the walls. Scars formed when the pine rasum had seeped from the wall boards and treked downward in awkward drizzles.

The crystalization of my concept about how walls **should not look** came later, however. It solidified when we moved to the Pugh Place. Now I don't blame the folks who lived there before us for doing what they did. With the wind blowing like a gale through the wide cracks in the walls it was the only thing they could have done.

The former tenants had taken little screen tacks and nailed every sheet of newspaper or every page of *Country Gentleman* magazine they could rake or scrape, they had nailed them all upon the walls. It was a frantic effort, I feel, to save themselves from freezing to death in the wintertime. And they had also availed themselves of the insulation of every proferred calendar from the City Drug or the Mercantile for the preceding ten years. They had collected them all upon ten penney nails at eye level throughout the Pugh house.

While we lived in that house I'd sit and read from the old yellowed papers about Mr. Mobley's daughter going off to finishing school in Europe or about Mr. Jack Drake taking the train into New York the previous summer. And I'd wonder about the taste of *Coca - Cola* or if *Cardui* could really do the things for women that the calendars said it could.

And I'd dream about the big house up the way that was painted. Painted a lovely white both inside and out. Every single wall bright and white, such a lovely cheery world in which to live. With no newsprint or huge calendar pictures messing up their walls. And I begged God to someday let me live in a house with wonderful, beautiful white walls — yards and yards of the spacious, magnificient empty walls.

And guess what! By His goodness I **now** live in a home with white walls both inside and out. And I've withstood my hubby for years over his notion of putting up interior paneling that resembles old pine walls.

And now comes these well - intentioned friends suggesting that I gather from the far corners of the earth every conceivable picture, object, and gadget and suspend them on my walls to obstruct my view of the gorgeous white walls I've dreamed about, longed for, and finally been blessed with. **Not on their lives.** (But I try to be kind to my friends. For as the young folks would say, "Most of my friends just don't know where I'm coming from.")

Now don't **you** get any ideas. Don't come snooping around to see if I'm telling the truth. Because I'm so happy to be able to see out windows which aren't stuffed with old pillows or which don't have boards nailed over them due to insufficient money to replace the broken windowpanes. I'm so thrilled over viewing the wide world from my bedroom windows that I'm not very keen on hanging curtains either.

Sit On Your Fist And Lean Back On Your Thumb

A saying once frequently used, especially by my smart - alec brother, was "Sit on your fist and lean back on your thumb." For instance on cold winter nights when I'd enter the front room, find all available chairs taken, and wail, "Where'm I gonna sit?" — well, then my brother Bill'd pop off, "Just sit on your fist and lean back on your thumb."

To be honest with you, chairs were so scarce when I was a kid until at times it would seem like a fist was the only available resting place. The four, six straight chairs we owned were wobbly things with sagging bottoms or else had makeshift cushions concealing rough boards that'd been nailed across their frames to compensate for the worn - out caning. These straight chairs, nontheless, were our recliners.

Well, when Daddy and Mr. Homer sat on the porch on rainy Sunday afternoons and speculated about the wet spell — well, the men then reclined their straight chairs against the slate grey wall of the weathered porch. And sometimes when I started to sit in a chair which Bill had previously spied out — well, just as I 'sat' Bill snatched, and I, consequently, 'reclined' on the floor.

The Wing Back of my day was half - a - nail - keg, one that had been hollowed out to become a small child's chair. Nail kegs were also the equivalent of today's bar stools; the main difference being the splinters along the keg's sides which quickly taught folks never to wrap their legs around the stools. Plus the kegs were utilized for sitting throughout the house, at all times, not just for eating. Mama once fancied a keg up with a tie-dyed cushion and skirt to grace a fancy apple crate dressing table for my sister and me.

A baby's high chair, when I was a kid, consisted of a straight chair whose board bottom had been heightened with two old Sears and Roebuck Catalogues. Or into whose sagging lap a small rocker had been placed, converting it into a citified high chair like the booster chairs now available for children in restaurants.

Once a child was old enough to begin eating mashed peas it was tied into such a high chair with a guano sack towel and was scooted up to the table between Mama and Daddy so they could alternate mashing the peas and poking them into the baby's mouth.

While the baby was sitting in his cattylog high chair, long ago, most of the other siblings sat around the table on long, backless benches. The benches were very rough when first constructed. But over years of use the kids' backsides robbed the benches of their splinters, rendering them smooth and worthy of exhibit in many homes today as family heirlooms.

True, there was a shortage of comfortable chairs at our house when I was growing up. But this never seemed to bother us. When we gathered in the front room, the fireplace room, after supper during the wintertime, we kids were happy to opt for sitting on the edge of the two double beds instead of in the straight chairs or the one rocker near the hearth. Of course we were colder back there but the ones up around the fire were usually huddled over a tub of corn, shelling it for the mill on Saturday.

We didn't know to be distraught over not owning a hide - a - bed or a comfy sectional. Come to think of it we did have a sectional sofa once. Mama made it by building a crude wooden frame, adding half of a set of bed springs, and topping it with a cotton - filled guano sack mattress. After she tie - dyed a guano sack cover for it, the sofa was quite fancy. But it was seldom sat upon since it was positioned off in the cold room across the hall.

And in a roundabout way we had a hide-a-bed; it was the quilt box. When company came we opened the lid and took out the beds for company. That is, we took out the extra quilts and made pallets on the floor in order to have sleeping space for all guests. When they went home we again hid the beds in the box.

Posteriors of my generation were acclimated to sitting on surfaces different from today's softies. When the nail keg's metal rim — which stood about one inch above the wooden surface — when it was not softened by a cushion it dug into kids' fannies. And at every spare moment young boys careened wildly down steep hillsides, the mendits in their leaky washpan seats hitting paydirt everytime their truck wagon's wooden tires rotated.

Young girls sat on sofas they'd created out of dreams and pine straw in the pastures. And courting couples sat on their Mama's wash benches down at the spring on Sunday afternoons. Men, meanwhile, sat on chopblocks out at the woodpile, or they hunched, leaned or squatted rather than reclining on sofas watching ball, like nowadays.

Maybe those tough seats made real men out of the males back then. For as they gathered thusly, visiting, on Sunday afternoons and discussed their fields which were dry as dustbowls or grassed over like hair on a dog's back — regardless of the sad state of their crops which they discussed they never left their visiting and worked in the fields. They never took the Lord's Day for that; they saved it for Him.

The inventor of today's Bean Bag, I believe, was one like myself who'd had cotton piled on his front porch, awaiting ginning. And he'd always enjoyed lazing, slouching, and even sleeping on it. So he gave this present generation a socially acceptable version of a cotton pile with its seeds intact — the bean bag in designer fabrics.

Yep, sittin' gear, as my Daddy called it, was in short supply awhile back, but then we weren't uptight about paying for it either. So if hard times come your way and you can't make the loan payments on your Wing Backs, Recliners and Plush Sofas — just do what the old timers did. Grab a wobbly straight chair, a nail keg, or a chopblock. Or just "Sit on your fist and lean back on your thumb."

Let The Young'uns Make Frog Houses

Adam and I are in agreement: young'uns should be permitted to make frog houses instead of bustin' a gusset to compete in Little League baseball.

The surprising thing about this unusual meeting - of - the - minds is that I'm a card carrying AARP member and Adam is my eight year - old grand - nephew. Consider also that I grew up when building frog houses was in vogue whereas Adam is a product of the computer generation. Nevertheless, I think the young man has hit on something which will set him apart in this fast world, in more ways than one.

Adam is finding contentment in his own neck of the woods, being happy just catching lightning bugs late on a spring day instead of catching balls with the boys down at the field. Choosing the simple recreation has already put the little boy in a different compartment. It has caused both young and old to question if he is a sissy.

He and I like being unusual if that's what it takes to call up doodle bugs. "Doodle bug, doodle bug, your house is on fire! Come out! Come out!" we call as we take our fingers and go round 'n round in the miniature volcanoes all over the sandy part of the yard. We know that by our calling and digging in the flour - soft soil at the same time the tiny little bugs will soon pop out.

When we have the doodle bugs called up we start fishing for 'jacks.' We take slender blades of grass with a little water - spit on them — once these simple fishing poles are dangled into the little round holes dotting the driveway they will produce jacks. Jacks are the funny inch - long worms with horns on their heads whose only purpose in life has always been to amuse little boys like Adam by clinging onto proffered grasses or broomstraws.

Having the ingenuity to weave your own

original suit out of huge cowcumber leaves, using small twigs for both needle and thread — tailoring your own outfit down by the creek as I did as a child, and having the fortitude to wear the stinging, fuzzy thing — well, this'll take more of a man than donning the identical uniform as twenty other little fellers on a ballfield.

And what about eating your sister's mud pies? And searching for arrow heads. Looking for flint rocks, bursting them open, and experimenting with the beautifully colored powders inside? Or being able to differentiate between a tumble bug who makes his home in the barnyard and the June bug from the garden with it's green sheen?

Having the dexterity and gentleness required to loop a sewing thread around a June bug's leg and then to 'fly' him like a kite for hours — well, these pursuits aren't for the simple - minded or the jelly - hearted, either. Adam's grandmother, my sister and illustrator, Trillie, found that out as a child. Trillie's strung - up June bug got swallowed by one of Mama's best laying hens. The chicken turned up dead of a mysterious ailment a few days later and left Trillie with a nagging, man - sized problem: "Would she come clean, just spill the beans to Mama or continue to remain silent and bear the heavy guilt?"

Then there's working with clay; another

leisure pastime Adam prefers over the rush and bustle of Little League, traveling miles to play this team or that. This little fellow who is nimble - fingered with a video game or a computer, however, is not into colored modeling clay. He likes to do like Bill and I did as kids back in the 30s — dig that clay - sand mixture out of the creekbed and work with it for hours — pounding, kneading, washing until it is clean, pure clay, ready for molding into something unique and beautiful. Great craftsmen have been doing the same thing for centuries.

This boy, whose name is the same as God's first man, is also content to just take walks with his family. To find little 'head - knockers' in the fall of the year — the little round balls on the end of sticks that are located near the Black - Eyed Susan patches. Adams likes to tease his little sister Jessica by tapping gently on her head with these. And he likes to run ahead and locate a paw - paw bush so he and his sister can sing and act out —

> *"Picking up paw - paws,*
> *puttin' 'em in your pocket,*
> *Picking up paw - paws,*
> *puttin' 'em in your pocket,*
> *Picking up paw - paws,*
> *puttin' 'em in your pocket,*
> *Way down yonder in the paw - paw patch."*

The nature - loving boy and I have even more in common. We like to come upon a patch of dandelions, all puffy, air - like. And fan them back and forth, and watch their little parachuting seeds go gliding through the sky, off to some place we make - believe about.

To sneak up quickly on those unsuspecting, fern - like plants and with one quick touch make them fold their leaves like a baby's eyelids dropping suddenly in slumber. Then stand there, taunting the tightly closed plant with, "Sleepy head, sleepy head, wake up, sleepy head!"

The gentle child and I both delight in making 'cows' from overgrown squashes and cucumbers, in shooting chinnie - berries through a home - make pop - gun, the kind my Dad taught my brother Bill to fashion as a kid. In drawing chickens in the sand like my Granny Porter did.

Now I'll concede that good things have happened to many kids who've been channeled into Little League by the time they turned four. Some have blossomed under the keen competition and the physical exercise of the game. But it's not for everyone. You'll never make me believe that my son's character was strengthened as he wept uncontrollably following his first Little League game, devastated that his weeks of dedicated practice all ended on the bench because his coach had only one goal — WIN!

Long ago when a thunderstorm ran us from the fields we'd take advantage of the wet sand in the yard. From the oldest to the youngest at the time — little Donald still in apron - dresses and hippin's (diapers) — we all got into the act of covering each other's bare feet with soothing, wet sand. After the soil was firmly packed over the toes and as far back as the legs permitted — then came the tricky part, that of gently sliding one's foot out the back way in order to leave intact a little fragile sand - cave.

As dusk came on we'd sometimes discover toads underneath the bushes and whisk them off to those newly erected frog houses. Oh, the creatures never took up residence therein. But we'd had fun together as a family group; that was the important thing. And my older brother Bill didn't turn out to be a sissy from participating in the calming activity. Served his country with valor and courage during thick and thin in both Korea and Viet Nam. Then retired only to make a second career of teaching, turning boys into men down at the vocational school.

In these times when even small children are often in a constant rush — when the little fellers are prone to nervous tensions, personality disorders, and ulcers at an early age — I say let Adam and other young'uns have a little leisure time. Let them make cucumber cows or frog houses in the backyard. It'll help them come to grips with God, with nature, and with eating their sister's mud pies.

Puffin' On Corn Silks, Cross Vines, And Rabbit Toback'r

AND WATCHING OUTTA THE CORNER UV MY EYE FER MAMA

Long ago when the drudgery of the day's chores seemed overwhelming we kids revolted against our parents' wishes for us, like kids have always done. When cleaning out the chicken house, slopping the hogs, and picking cotton on the back forty got crossways in our craw, we'd vow to do something drastic.

We ruled out cussin' cause Mama'd know about it and wash our mouths out with soap. There was no way of gettin' into town and no money to go wild with iffen we'd uv got there. The only avenue of rebellion left to us — with a little daring to it — was to sneak around and smoke a little.

Our Daddy smoked. Smoked ready rolls if he could ever in a blue moon afford a pack. Next in line to his heart was a can of Prince Albert Smoking Tobacco with a nickel pack of nice thin OCB papers to roll the toback'r in. But usually times were so hard he had to settle for a little bag of *Country Gentleman*. And had to get by with using a piece of brown paper poke or part of a page from the *Country Gentleman* magazine to roll it in.

Daddy hated that. The magazine or poke paper would burn quickly, often burning his lips in the process. And since it wouldn't seal together like the thin tissues of OCB it would often spill his precious toback'r, sometimes the very last smoke between him and the rolling store the following day.

When Daddy ran completely out of cigarette makings, it was rough on everybody. So we were glad when the insurance man came to call and Daddy swallowed his pride and said, "How about bumming a colby from ye?"

But Daddy's smoking seemed a big thing to us; something we wanted to copy, especially Bill. Wanted to try our luck at when the trials of the day were going against the grain, even though we knew Mama was dead set against it.

So when Bill decided to be a Big Ike he gathered some of the velvety gray leaves from the wild rabbit tobacco plant down in the pasture, got 'em in the fall when they were getting all dried up-like. And I, slouching around behind him like his shadow, followed him to the barn.

Out there he rolled the leaves 'round 'n 'round in his hand 'til they started to look like Daddy's *Country Gentleman*. Then he took out a piece of brown paper poke, make a little trough in it, filled it with the rabbit toback'r and rolled 'er up. With the match he had snitched from the house he was soon puffing away, just like Daddy. 'Cept he was doing a lot of coughing and choking; but even then he looked real growed - up a'doin' it. Oh, I'se so proud uv 'im but I didn't have the gumption to try it. Not jest then.

Another day Bill got him some corn silks outta a couple o' dried ears of corn. Made a co'by outta them just like he'd done with the rabbit toback'r. And puffed it when we were over clearing the new ground, just me and him, no little 'uns along to tell Mama.

And he tried his luck at smoking cross vines down in the bottom one day. 'Lowed how they'd really 'bit' his tongue, lots worse than the other two toback'rs he'd tried.

Finally, I couldn't stand it any longer. So 'bout dark one evenin,' when Bill and I were all tuckered out from pulling that old crosscut saw backards and forwards, I said to him, "Wanna smoke a little rabbit toback'r? I've got two matches from the box offen the kitchen wall, some brown poke, and some toback'r from the edge uv the field."

"Speck so," he said.

So we slithered up under the high part of the house, up under the kitchen. And we lit up and I started in 'a trying my first smoke. Somehow it jest didn't taste as good as I had figured it would. And d'rectly I started coughing, but not real loud, 'cause I handed the cigarette to Bill and held my hand over my mouth.

Didn't help matters though. 'Cause 'bout that time the kitchen door opened and Mama hollered, "Nonie Faye, you and Bill git yourselves from under th' kitchen 'a smoking that rabbit toback'r this minute! And I don't mean maybe! Bring a load of wood 'a piece and get yourselves into this house."

Mama didn't say much more, except to ask iffen we didn't think she could smell that stinking stuff a mile off. I think perhaps it was because she saw how green I was soon looking around the gills. I didn't even want any of her fried sweet 'taters for supper, the thing that I usually loved. She 'lowed Bill and I had to wash the dishes *ever'* night for a week. And only the Lord himself knows how I made it though that night's washing, before I fell into bed, sick as a dog.

I was cured on smoking for a couple of years. Then I saw pictures in a *True Romance* magazine of girls smoking a ready - roll. Looked so fancy, them being Bette Davis look - alikes, and having such handsome boys with 'em. And then one day Daddy got a pack of *Lucky Strike* ready - rolls. When he laid 'em out on the dresser that night I sneaked one.

Got my chance the next afternoon. Got sent, all alone, down to the spring to bring up the clothes. Grabbed my cigarette and a couple o' matches and ran all the way down the long, winding hill. Lit up and started smoking. Was determined to blow smoke back out of my mouth like I'd seen Daddy do. Had heard someone say you had to swallow the smoke first, however.

I puffed, sucked in, and swallowed. I tried to blow out but no luck. I did this over and over, about five times. By then I was coughing like I had TB or the consumption. And my throat felt as hot as I figured Hell'd be, 'a burning and 'a stinging to beat the band. (And I **WAS** thinking 'a lot about Hell, and damnation, and my own punishment for the sins I'd just committed that day.)

I stomped that cigarette to the smithereens! Started praying. And telling God how sorry I was. And started drinking from the spring. I musta 'bout drank that spring nearly dry, stayed down there 'til it was dusky dark. Then went in home sick'ern a horse. Last time I ever, ever wanted to "puff, puff, puff, that cigarette." Felt I'd had my punishment from the Good Lord, too.

More than four decades have come and gone since Bill smoked corn silks, cross vines, and rabbit toback'r, And since the Lord dealt severely with me when I stole that *Lucky Strike* and disobeyed Mama by smoking. I met sisters recently who confessed that they, too, took part in smoking some wild weeds long ago.

Seems Grace and her siblings were into smoking cross vines even though it hurt their tongues bitterly. Now, living across from the church as they did, they discovered accidentally that the vine handles on some of the church's funeral parlor fans were made of cross vines. They further realized that dried cross vines were the best kinds to smoke.

So they took to sneaking over to the church and taking the handles off the fans. Slipping the cross vines, if you please, to take out into the thicket and puff 'em. Seems those ladies, like myself, have had to do some confessing to the Lord over the years. Confessing about causing all those hot folks to have to try to fan on

Sundays using fans without handles.   And vowing, like Bill and I did — after Mama caught us smoking under the kitchen floor — that we were gonna quit puffing on corn silks, cross vines, and that good ole rabbit toback'r.

My Mama's An Unusual Bag Lady

Folks nowadays think of a *bag lady* as a poverty - stricken woman whose meager earthly treasures are all in a bag which she guards hourly with her very life. In one sense of the word my Mama would've fit into the above category four decades back. But then again — she was not, nor is she yet — your typical bag woman.

As the wife of a red - dirt tenant farmer with ten little 'uns to feed during the Great Depression Mama would have today been classified, by the government, as 'in the poverty category'. However, she never viewed herself as needful of charity, probably because she **was** a *bag lady*.

To be truthful, her early treasures were largely 'tied up in bags', not one, but many. In fact her very existence, and that of her family as well, revolved around the bags. And our lives were charted 'a - right because she was very wise in regard to the bags that came into her life.

The most important bags, because of their sheer numbers, to come into my Mama's life were the guano bags or sacks. Yep, those rough cotton bags, in which fertilizer for the cotton, corn, and vegetable crops were purchased, formed the bag backbone in Mama's life.

After they were washed in strong lye soap and bleached in the May sun and dew, Mama transformed them into undergarments, outer garments, bath linens, sofa covers, quilt linings — you name it, she utilized the guano sacks for it.

After the peach and apple slices — intimidated by that old extrovert, the sun — after the timid pieces had shrunken almost into obscurity, Mama raked the shriveled bits from their hot tin bed and into either a clean guano or a 48 lb. flour sack. Week after hot week this process was repeated, until the relief of fall arrived.

Then Mama's treasured fruit bags were tied tightly about and suspended, by means of a wire, from the rafters of the lean - to bedroom. There they hung, tempting me until dried - fruit - pie- time on cold days. The wires made it impossible for a vagrant field mouse to attack the cotton sacks and, thusly, the precious dried fruit.

On warm autumn days dried peas and beans were thrashed per Mama's directions. Actually, very little beating with the brushbroom stubs was required. For all summer long as any dried legumes had been spied in the garden, Mama had made sure they found their way into their respective guano or crocker sacks. The latter burlap bags — with their coarsely woven, stingy fabric, were great for sunning the giant, drying fordhood limas.

As the tied bags were placed daily in the hot summer - fall sunshine, from inside the bags could often be heard the "snap", "pop", as the vegetable hulls curled and released their seeds voluntarily.

After the formal thrashing, however, came the separation of the chaff. A sheet made of guano sacks was placed outside, on clean sand in the yard. The legumes were poured down slowly on a windy day, permitting the breeze to whisk away the hull pieces and the fuzz. The remaining hard - as - rock peas and beans were then tied into clean guano sacks or into the finer grade cotton sugar bags, the ones in which we'd bought 100 lbs. of sugar for making preserves and jellies. Mama saw to it that the dried vegetables bags then became next - door, or next - rafter, neighbors to the dried fruit bags.

And more *bag neighbors* were on their way. After we'd climbed into the barn loft on cold Saturday afternoons and picked peanuts off the vines and into guano sacks, these also took their place on the lean - to rafters. And then came the shelled popcorn, hiding from hungry mice and youngsters. (For shame, for shame — one time I went up to get parching peanuts and took, instead, those earmarked *seed peanuts*; planting was very skimpy the following year.)

Mama utilized even the tiniest of bags. One cloth salt bag became a button bag, a place of necessity and also one which furnished hours of endless pleasure, looking at Mama's wondrous collection of both common and beautiful buttons.

Small bags often became things of beauty. Salt bags were just the correct size for handkerchiefs; they took on a whole new look with Mama's fancy embroidery and tatting added. Once Mama helped me transform several 48 lb. flour sacks into a prize - winning 4 - H Club dress. When completed with drawn work and dyed with yellow Rit it won out over many beautiful dresses sewn with store - bought printed material.

And now, a half - century after Mama stitched it for me, my bed boasts a Lone Star Quilt whose white squares were cut, by the Bag Lady, from tiny Country Gentleman Tobacco sacks.

But of all bags, perhaps the most used was

Mama's rag bag. Kept in a convenient place and filled with scraps of old clothing or worn pieces from other bags, this bag was called upon to **provide** many times daily. From it we'd snatch a dishrag, a wash rag (bath cloth), a dusting rag, a headrag (a scarf to wear out to the barn to milk Ole Bossy on a freezing morning), a rag to bind up an injured foot. And on and on the trips to Mama's rag bag continued.

Years ago Mama took advantage of bags which others did not want and made useful, beautiful things for her family from them. Many were my dresses from feed bags, or sacks, which the neighbors or relatives did not have a need for. Back in the 40s my Uncle Doc gave Mama countless burlap bags from horse feed; these were washed and boiled, then transformed into a warm filling for comforters.

And Mama, the bag woman, never tires of bags; her life is still tied to her bags. I stopped by the home of this white - haired, 82 year old on a hot day in 1989. She sat at her sewing machine buried under piles of 40 - 50 year old guano sacks. These were bags which she had just inherited; her Aunt Lizzie had gone to her reward and left them. There Mama sat, enduring her arthritic pain, making Christmas aprons from the antique cotton bags — truly an atypical Bag Lady if there's ever been one!

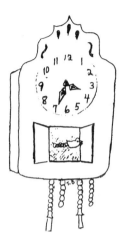

Chancing It On
A Punchboard
MORE EXCITING THAN A LOTTERY

You might say that Eve took a chance when eating the forbidden fruit, just after the world's creation. And, I reckon, ever since that time games of chance have been around, right down to the present day computerized, state - operated lotteries. But if I were a gambler I'd be willing to wager that today's gimmicks don't hold a light — in the amount of fun — to those making the rounds when Mama and I came along. Nope, lotteries just can't hold a candle to cake walks, box suppers, nor punchboards.

During the thirties fate smiled on my friend Earnestine: let the letter carrier leave her a punchboard. The Grand Prize to be had was a Cuckoo Clock. And Earnestine's reward, her compensation for the work, was to be a genuine, one - hundred - percent silk scarf to tie her head up with instead of the flour sack one she was then using.

Earnestine's Mama tried to talk some sense into her, tried to get her to tear the little pasteboard game into pieces. Told her how much trouble it'd be to collect all the money. But that high - spirited gal was bound - 'n - determined to wear that fancy headrag. She brought the punchboard to school every day, sneaked around behind the teachers' backs, bragged about that clock with the little bird that'd run out and in again.

Earnestine was tempting us to take a chance on something we just couldn't afford. Saying things like, "You'll probably punch out a circle that'll only cost a penny! And just think — you'll have a chance on that big prize!"

With talk like that my friend had the town kids going without their hot lunches just to push out little circles with Peg, Sal, Meg, and other names printed on them. Those same names were listed on the back of the board, with space alongside them for listing the names of those who

did the punching. The list of names became a
quick reference for the big prize. And some
boards also awarded smaller prizes to four, five
folks.

But the biggest surprise of all was tucked
inside the circles which were punched out. For
printed there between the cardboard was the
amounts of money to be paid: they ranged from
one cent to forty - nine cents.

Kids at school and neighboring adults
made all sorts of sacrifices in order to take a
chance on that Cuckoo Clock. Miss Lizzie sold an
old hen to the rolling store to *pay up* after
punching out a tiny circle with 'thirty - nine cents'
hidden inside: she 'lowed how grand that clock
was gonna look over her mantel.

Jimbo, a twelfth grader, punched out five
circles while riding home on the school bus; said
he had his mind set on "giving that Cuckoo Clock
to Lillie Bell for her hope chest." (We all knew he
had his mind set on sharing Lillie Bell's hope
chest one sweet day.)

Unlucky Jimbo ended up having to skip
school and skid logs to pay the two dollars and
twenty - nine cents he owed Earnestine for the
breath - taking excitement of five chances. And
me—well, please don't tell Mama that I sneaked
and sold half - a - dozen brown eggs to my
teacher to pay the eighteen cents that glared me
in the face when my common sense gave way to

covetousness.

And poor Earnestine. Had to hound folks for two months before she could mail the money in. During that time she lost fifteen cents and recklessly spent sixty cents of others' money on herself; had to sell the forthcoming silk scarf to Ina Lou for an advancement of the seventy - five cents which she was indebted.

As bad luck would have it, after all chances had been pushed from the punchboard — and on **the day** when a slew of excited, hopefuls crowded around and watched Earnestine punch out the one big circle with the winning name — well, as luck would have it, the feller who lived in the *big house* and who owned a grandfather clock that reached from floor to ceiling — well, he won the little cuckoo clock.

But we didn't learn our lesson. The very next time someone received a punchboard in the mail — with a grand prize of a battery - operated *Philco* radio — well we all went crazy as bessie bugs trying to figure out how to beat the odds and how to get the money to pay for a chance on *getting something for nothing.*

And when they had the Halloween Carnival at school every year we did the same thing. Paid all the money we had in this world just to walk around and around in a circle. Wagered our entire five cents on the hope that the feller facing into the corner would stop playing his 'juice' (Jew's) harp when we were standing on the lucky square. Figured we'd then be on our way to riches, what with winning the four - layered - hikker - nut cake.

Or else we'd pay to guess the number of grains of corn in a gallon jug. Or to speculate on what was placed underneath the slices of a chocolate pie. There was just something about taking a chance that got our blood to boiling, that set our sap to rising. Of course, when Bro. Wilcutt came and held the revival underneath the brush arbor he called "taking a chance on getting something for nothing, called it **sin, gambling**." Said God was "agin it." Said betting on rooster fights was wrong, too. And even box suppers.

I figure Cordie Mae, now pushing ninety - two years, would agree with the Reverend. Well, she'll tell you in a flash — like she did me recently — of her experience with a box supper when she was sweet sixteen.

Seems the Bell Buckle School put on a box supper to raise money to buy coal for heating the school the following winter. Now Cordie Mae's heart was all a - flutter for John Tom, the young handsome feller from the Who'd - A - Thought - It Community. So she set about hand - embroidering a napkin to put inside a little basket. And on the day of the Box Supper — well, the young lady baked cookies, and buttermilk biscuits, and made fried apple pies, and fried up chicken, and deviled eggs — you name it, Cordie Mae had it in that basket.

And Cordie Mae also pointed the basket out to John Tom who arrived at the shindig prepared to spend his entire month's salary of five dollars on the basket, if need be. It would be a gesture on his part to let the whole wide world know that the beautiful brunette in the new checkered dress and bonnet was "his gal."

But as the Reverend under the brush arbor pointed out "taking a chance just never pans out." And Cordie Mae watched with disbelief that night as the town's half - wit took a filthy tobacco sack filled with silver dollars from his hind pocket and out - bid everyone else. He paid an unbelievable thirty dollars for her basket and for the privilege of eating supper with her.

Some were later heard to say, "Well, it went for a good cause." But my friend recently echoed the preacher by saying, "The end doesn't always justify the means."

Politicians nowadays are saying our state is just never gonna be able to pay for quality education without a state lottery. And seems as if I recall that just a few years back, when they were making their pitch for the legalization of dog racing and horse racing, — seems they billed that also as a cure - all for the ills of the poor and underprivileged and a panacea for education.

It just hasn't happened, however. Instead

we've found out, like Earnestine, that too often it's the feller up "in the Big House" who wins the bet, or the lottery. Even the computers tell us you have only one chance in every eight million of winning the lottery when you play.

Seems we'd wake up and see it like Cordie Mae and the Reverend; that the end is just not worth the means. But if we can't come to our senses — and if we've just gotta resort to some sort of state - endorsed gambling — I say, "Forget the lottery and go with punchboards! They excite more folks, stretch out the suspense, and give away those wonderful Cuckoo Clocks!"

Bill's Hankering For The Ole Wash Hole

Long ago on Sunday afternoon of the first really hot weekend of summer we kids knew it was time to shape up the ole wash hole. With the morning's church behind us and no chores allowed on the Lord's Day, we'd meander down to the shallow creek, intent on re - creating our swimming pool, the one that winter rains with their stolen topsoil had filled in.

We were an odd lot as we began our crusade. Bill in his ragged cut - off overalls and we girls in our shortest ever'day dresses tackled the rearranging of the rocks in the creek bed to make a dam. After the rocks were in place we'd begin chinking the cracks between them with sand, topsoil, and even clay that we scooped and dug from the creek bed with our bare hands. We left a small opening on one side, an outlet for the water to escape downstream, while we worked; the buildup of the water would come later.

What joy and exhilaration when some of Bill's friends showed up bringing shovels and hoes! We'd all work feverishly then, digging the deepening hole ever deeper and securing the dam higher and thicker and stronger. Sometimes the big boys would lug huge rocks from the hillsides for reinforcements. And we all were alert for the sight or the feel of any sharp rocks underfoot that might later cause a wader to end up with a cut foot or leg.

It took more than one afternoon to build a really secure dam. So we worked unyieldingly at the wash hole ever minute we could steal. Sometimes the rain'd keep us from field work and we'd be allowed to run down to the creek for a spell. And occasionally, just by sheer luck, we'd knock off the field work and get barnyard chores completed twenty minutes before dark. When this happened we'd fly down the hill, to our self-appointed construction of a summer recreational facility.

The work was hard and would today be classified as back - breaking labor but to us it was pure pleasure — a means to a wonderful end. And we had fun in the going, as well. To reward ourselves as we worked, we occasionally sloshed around in the shallow water. And Bill'd surprise us by quickly dashing a wall of water onto us by means of his two strong hands joined together. If the water began to rise in the hole, and if none of Bill's friends were around, we girls would tuck our dress tails into our Mother's Best Self - Rising floorsack bloomers while we romped with Bill.

Finally the day would come when the break in the dam was filled in and the ole wash hole was allowed to fill up. This was exciting and we girls enjoyed being there as the water rose. However, when it had reached it's optimal depth it was often too deep for us to wade in and none of us knew how to swim. So for the most part, the deep wash hole became a 'boy's swimming and diving hole.'

It would lose that designation, however, when the heavy rains came and broke the dam, letting some of the water escape. Or on those rare Sunday afternoons when Mama and Daddy accompanied us to the creek and let us 'swim' with homemade life jackets.

The preservers were made by placing two empty gallon - molasses - buckets, with tightly - fitted lids, inside a clean fertilizer sack and then tying it together at the end. We positioned our chest on top of the sack, with one of the buckets on either side of our small bodies. This provided a means by which we non - swimmers could paddle all over the deep creek, under our parents' supervision, and have the time of our lives.

I really wanted to learn to swim but it seemed that everytime I thought of going to the creek to try, there would be Daddy, standing at the edge of the yard, hollering, "If you go off to that creek and come back here drowned, I'm gonna tear you up." I knew Daddy was a man of his word.

Looking back, fifty years later, I realize that I might have learned if I had followed the route that my friend, Howard Smithson, chose. Seems when 'Howie' was struggling to learn to swim, the older boys at the swimming hole 'helped him out.' They cut a 'float' out of a fish and instructed the young boy to "Swallow this and you'll be able to swim, swim just like a fish." So trusting Howie put the one and one - half inch inflated bubble into his mouth and gulped. Down it went. And sure enough — after being sick for twenty - four hours, and then after much effort at the swimming hole, my friend reports he **did** learn how to swim.

Long ago when the water was too deep down at the wash hole for us girls to wade, we would still beg to tag along, just to watch Bill and his friends.   The boys had found a heavy wild grapevine dangling from a tall tree near the deepest point of the water. They had cut the vine to within three, four feet of the ground. From there they took turns — Bill, Gene, Bobby, Edward, Bill, . . . As the dark haired muscular one grabbed the vine and let it carry him back and forth a few times in ever widening circles we'd start yelling, "Look out below! He's gonna take a preacher's seat! Bobby's coming!" And then he'd turn lose the vine, jerk his knees to chest height and, circling his arms around his knees, he'd come down, fanny first, with a mighty splash into the water.

We would all scream, "Holy Cow! What a splash! Bet **you** can't do it that good, Gene!" Bobby would come up from underneath the water about that time, sputtering and swimming to the edge, anxious to run around and get in line again. Sometimes as the boys swung the vine in circles or as they left the vine they'd let out a blood - curdling "YYYEEEEeeeeeooooooooooo!" like they'd heard Tarzan do on a pictur' show in town, when the loin - clothed feller was swinging from vines in the jungle.

At times the boys "Double - Dog Dared" me and my sisters to tag along as they headed to the ole wash hole. On one such occasion I waited until they were out of sight and sneaked down to the creek, anyway, curious. There, hidden by the huge cowcumber leaves I, as a 10 year old girl, got my first sex education lesson. I saw my 12 year old brother jumping off the side of the bank in his birthday suit, doing "Belly Busters" (falling face - down into the water, on his naked belly). No need to explain that it took me less than a second to head back to the house. And I tried to hide my lack of surprise when Bill came home that night, complaining that his stomach was chapped.

After a girl got 12, 14 years old, back then, she didn't ask to go wading with her brother and his friends. Because she usually had a crush on one of the boys and would in no way let the boys see her in the water. Besides, the preacher warned that "mixed bathing" would bring us into hell fire and damnation.

Yes, the ole wash hole provided us with lots of fun long ago — and a place to cool off on hot, sultry days. It also provided us with an incentive to look out for nails; stick a rusty nail in your foot and you'd not be allowed in the water during 'dog days.' And although the water rushing from the hillside often left the wash hole muddy, we knew the water was pure; no chlorine was needed back then.

The hot days of summer are upon us again. Bill and I need a place to cool off, yet we shrink at today's water pollution and chlorine. And thinking of all the fun we had in by - gone years down at the creek, with me able to paddle around between the 'lasse buckets without embarrassment, Bill and I have a strong hankering for the ole wash hole!

When We Funeralized Ole Drum

My daily paper speaks of innovations for deceased pets: lavish caskets, perpetual care cemeteries, and stately funeral services. In their words, burial with dignity for Spot has **just arrived**.

Do I have news for them! When Bill and I, along with four other siblings, funeralized Daddy's ole redbone hound four decades back — when we laid Ole Drum to rest in the pine thicket out past the smokehouse, *Going in Style* was invented.

Now it was only fitting that we *put on the dog* (excuse the pun) for Ole Drum considering the family provider, friend, and protector that he'd been through the years. Yep, ever since Daddy'd gotten the fat pup from his brother Gray the hound'd been a hunter. That creature with the tummy as round and tight as a drum'd tree those squirrels faster'n any dog alive — provided flavorin' for many 'a dumplin' in his time, he did.

Saved our hides up there on that mountain more times than one. Let Daddy know when the panther was out in the barn, put off his siren when the mad dog was nearing our yard and little tottler Doug, and 'twas Drum who bore the brunt of seven rattlesnakes' wrath while clearing out blackberry bushes for our picking.

Yep, when Drum went to meet his Maker beneath the wheels of a log truck after surviving all that rattlesnake venom it was only fitting that he be laid to rest like nobility. (And it grieves me that the plan we originated back then is now being copied by money grubbing pet cemeterians all over our country.)

The current news articles claim that heretofore pet owners have been embarrassed to grieve over the loss of their pets. They say, however, that modern grief therapists and support groups are helping folks deal with their Pet Loss

Syndrome. We didn't know to attach all those fancy labels back then, but like I said they've copied all the concepts from our funeralizing of Ole Drum.

When Bill came running home from the gravel road carrying the crushed, limp body of our dear pet in his arms tears were coursing down his cheeks. Soon the entire family was in sobs, Daddy and Mama included. (That was one time when Mama didn't wipe her eyes daintily with the hem of her apron and make remarks about gnats being in her eyes.) And amid their tears and sorrow Mama and Daddy became our grief therapists, answering our questions about Dogs' Heaven and such. And right then and there our family formed a strong support group, the first perhaps for grief - stricken pet owners.

After awhile Daddy suggested, "Let's put Ole Drum out in the pine thicket. It'll be warm in the winter, away from the cutting winds, and cool in the summer, shaded from the hot sun." We all agreed it'd be a right fittin' place for the hard working hound to take his deserved rest.

While Bill and Daddy went with hoe and shovel to dig a deep rectangular hole, the rest of us concentrated on a fancy casket and shroud.

With reddened eyes Mama went to the smokehouse and got down the apple crate she'd planned to nail onto the kitchen wall for another dish cabinet. Then we girls gathered round while she got out her scrap sack. She felt the blue serge would be the most fitting. Mama said she'd heard once of a rich man's body being exhumed by thieves hunting his gold watch — dug up after forty years and his blue serge suit was still intact. Scared the thieves so badly, seeing that fine suit with crumbled bones in it — report was, she 'lowed, that they fled without looking for the gold watch.

So Mama gave us the remnants of Daddy's blue serge wedding suit from twenty years back — the remnants she'd planned to make herself a skirt from — these became Ole Drum's stately shroud. The blue, plus a bright red piece that was used to wrap his head, bonnet fashion, by the youngest of us at that time, little Doug.

After we'd lowered the rich wood casket into the grave and formed a mound with the fresh black earth, Daddy and Mama moseyed away; Mama to the house, Daddy toward the field. Neither of them mentioned that we kids should return to our work as they usually did. So we remained there to properly funeralize our dear departed friend.

We girls ran to the house to get our Sunday hankerchiefs with the embroidery on them so we could wipe our eyes and noses ladylike as we'd seen folks up at Pilgrim's Rest do when they layed Mr. Peters to rest. And we brought the Holy Bible for Bill. Everybody picked a bunch of Black - Eyed Susans and Touch - Me - Nots from the edge of the woods and stuck them upright in the fresh grave.

Bill climbed atop a stump near the burial site, opened the Bible, and started the sermon, "Breaaaaaatheeeeern . . . we're gathered to lay our dear friend to rest," he began in the manner of the Reverend.

We all stood quietly until we felt we should offer up some "AMEN" or "HALLELUJAH" when Bill shouted loudly about how God was "gonna reward Ole Drum's faithfulness with eternity in Dog Heaven!" He said, "God's gonna 'specially reward him the way he saved us from snakes, and the way he'd trot 'long behind the wagon's coupling pole and lick his tongue on my bare feet on the way home from the hot field."

Following this Bill said, "Sister Frances is gonna say a few words." (Actually Bill had to stop to cry a while). And then came the singing of dozens of songs. *We'll Meet You In The Morning, On Jordan's Stormy Banks I Stand, Amazing Grace, Home On The Ranch, Leaning On The Everlasting Arms, Oh, Suzanna, The Little Brown Church In The Wildwood* and on and on and on. We ate up the rest of the day funeralizing our dear Ole Drum in a proper manner.

I say **let** the modern International Association of Pet Cemeterians brag about their their fancy plastic caskets, and their landscaped gardens with fountains and statues of St. Francis of Assisi for the burial of deceased pets — I will **always maintain** that a pet was never interned with more style and decorum than when we funeralized Ole Drum in the pine thicket out past our smokehouse. And certainly never with more love.

Daddy's Old Wagon
Was A Good'un
IT HELD ITS OWN WHEN
THE MULES GOT SPOOKED

Daddy's old wagon was simply that, "Old." It was second, perhaps even third - hand, when obtained as part of the equipment necessary for eking out a living from the land upon which we were thrust during the Great Depression. The wagon consisted of a shaky, pine - timbered box atop an aging, but still - strong axle, tongue, and four wooden - wheeled foundation. It came as part of a package deal with the mules, stubborn Ole Frank and his mate, gentle Pat.

If Daddy's wagon had ever boasted a coat of shiny red paint you couldn't tell it when it came our way. It was then a weathered gray with some of the decaying parts held together, here and there, by pieces of rusted hay - baling wire. Even the wagon bed was wired in places, as was some of the hardware on the tongue and the double - tree.   The latter, however, was eventually repaired by a trip to Grandpa's Porter's little blacksmithing operation.

But during hot, dry summers the only solution for the floppy metal rims on the wagon wheels was to wire them. To wire them until we could spare the time to soak the wheels in the creek's edge.   That, in time, would cause the wood to swell and again fit the rims.

Looking back fifty years I realize Daddy's old wagon was a symbolic item.   It came to be associated with security and love in my mind long ago, and remains so today.

The rough board nailed across Daddy's wagon bed up near the front was a far cry from the sophisticated spring seats on some wagons of that day.   It was even further removed from the plush seat of my Uncle Ferman's 'Hoover Buggy,' a vehicle my Dad's baby brother had made by converting the chassis and seat of his fancy T - Model Ford car into a mule - drawn wagon when gas became unobtainable during the Depression years.

But that sagging seat at the front of my Daddy's wagon was a place of happiness and love for me as a wee tot.   At first I rode there in Mama's arms, then sat upon her lap. Later I was afforded a place to sit - stand between Daddy's legs; there I was cushioned from the seat's splinters by the ragged quilt Mama always folded thereon for long rides.   From that enviable position Daddy'd let me hold the reins and drive Ole Frank and Pat as he lazily clucked to them while returning from a trip to Granny's on a Sunday afternoon.

As a truth, more times than not traveling in the wagon WAS a time for gently clucking to the old mules; usually a time for a relaxed, unhurried going.   The pace therein was not at all like the times when Daddy had the mules hooked to a stump in the new ground; there he'd be yelling and hollering to make them pull at their utmost strength.   Nor was it akin to the seasons, plowing around the tender vegetables in the garden, when Daddy's scream sharply, "WHOA, FRANK, WHOA, I TOLD YE, GEE!" I felt Daddy was not to blame for his impatience then, fearful as he was over a huge hoof crushing a fine tomato plant and having Mama upset.

But trips in the wagon were for fun and pleasure it seemed. Our way of getting from here to there, and from there to here, relaxed. Trips to church and back, even at night traveling along a precipitous road, were slow, happy times. There was always a load of friends in the wagon on such trips; whomsoever we spied just heading out from home a'foot or already walking along the dusty road — was invited to "Hop in" or "Hang on," onto the back of the wagon or onto the coupling pole. Moseying along Daddy would whistle, *Amazing Grace,* or we would all sing together, *Will the Circle Be Unbroken?* while the littlest babies slept on quilts in the wagon bed with the stars twinkling overhead.

Even returning home from the far field, late- of - a - day, was a relaxing trip. The wagon would be piled high with the fertilizer distributor, the cotton planter, grubbing hoes, buckets and guano sacks with their residue of 6 - 8 - 4. There'd be glass jugs drained of their last drop of tepid water, and the old pasteboard box emptied of its earlier contents of cooked 'taters and corn bread, our lunch over at the back forty. Tossed - aside sunbonnets would dot the entire scene as we, heading home in the wagon after a hard day, turned the wagon ride into leisure.

This became a time for Daddy to whistle softly and let the lines droop, to permit the mules to proceed at their own tired pace. And permit my siblings and me to sit on the coupling pole and drag our toes through the soothing sand of the road, resting ourselves for the evening chores then waiting at home.

A Saturday trip taking a wagon load of corn to the gristmill wasn't that rushed either. Nor the occasional trip into town and back on a Sat'dy for flour, coffee and a big stick of peppermint candy. Daddy knew the mules were exhausted from the week's work and didn't need whipping and rushing. It was a time for talking over the week's happenings and for commenting on the need for rain, or the blackness of the corn blades along the creek bottoms as the family rode slowly along in the wagon.

The times were few that Daddy's old wagon ever flew like the wind. One exception was when, as a 12 year old, Bill was holding the reins outside a grocery while Daddy was inside, peddling the fine produce they'd brought into the mining town. A young boy rode speedily by on his wheel (bicycle), spooking Ole Frank and Pat, causing them to bolt and run with the speed of light — or so it seemed to Bill as he and the good old wagon and the load of vegetables flew down the middle of Cordova. Only a brave man, stepping into the mule's path, halted the runaways and saved both Bill and Daddy's old wagon.

Another unusual strain on Daddy's wagon occurred the summer we had to outrun a quickly approaching rainstorm to get the hay into the barn. That old wagon cooperated grandly as we buzzed like bees — loading hay onto the V - shaped rack that had been placed down into the wagon bed, driving to the barn, throwing the foliage into the loft, driving, reloading, driving, unloading, driving, loading . . . Bill, at the reins while Daddy was away, drove furiously, like Jehu in the Bible as he flew in his chariot on the day when the Lord Almighty made a quick end to the evil King Ahab and Jezebel.   Unbelievably, Daddy's old wagon held up and the hay got in that day!

And, of course, there was the time when we drove Frances into town early one morning at a much more rapid clip than which the old mules were accustomed. Daddy didn't want his firstborn to be late for what was possibly the world's very first 'outpatient surgery.' The local doctor had announced a one - day clinic for the purpose of performing tonsillectomies on a whole passel of kids. Pat and Frank saw to it that Frances made it on time.

Yep, in a pinch Daddy's old wagon would stand up to the pressure of moving fast. And in so doing it came to represent our emergency vehicle, our ambulance — if you please. And a conveyance for rescue — when saving the hay. And to remind of a father's understanding assurance — after the mules ran away with Bill. These, plus the more usual, slow - paced uses of the old wagon which symbolized family unity, serenity, fun, relaxation, and neighborliness — all of these symbols earned Daddy's old wagon a revered, symbolic place in my memory forever.

Mama And The Whittling Doll

Today's mamas, tired after a long week's work and a Saturday morning of housecleaning, will drop their teenagers off at the mall then pick up a video to occupy the little ones, thus getting them all out of their hair. My Mama, exhausted from a week in the cotton patch and a morning over the washtub and rubboard, took a different route with her children. She pulled us all together for a Saturday afternoon of laughter and relaxation with her whittling doll.

The large doll which I'd received for Christmas in the third grade, the same doll whose cry had revealed to me that Christmas Eve at 9

PM that my Daddy was Santa's helper — that doll, with a little magic from Mama, became the main object for many - a - Sat'day afternoon's delight.

A straight chair with its sagging bottom, once padded with feather bed pillows and covered over with a guano sack sheet, was placed in the middle of the front room to become a royal throne for the doll. The commanding queen, peeling from a reckless night when I forgot and left her outside in the dew, was placed atop her throne to be royally attired. She was dressed in a flowing robe; actually a long - sleeved guano sack shirt of Daddy's was placed on the queen, backwards, with the sleeves hanging limply by her sides.

The younger, unsuspecting children were removed from the room while Mama assumed her post behind the chair. Hidden there by the flowing sheet, Mama reached her hands upwards through the queen's shirt - robe until her hands became those of the doll - queen, hands whose identity remained a secret beneath the shirt cuffs.

As the small children were ushered into the doll's presence two objects were carefully placed into the doll's hands by an older sibling of mine. First the doll was given a harmless case knife (table knife) to whittle with and secondly it was given something on which to whittle — a small stick of stovewood, a block of wood, or a pencil.

"Whittle!," was the simple command given the doll by one of us older kids to get the ball rolling. And so the doll began to move the case knife up and down, up and down along the stick of wood. Then someone would shout, "FASTER!" and the dolls' stub - of - hands underneath the cloth would fairly fly. And as they did the younger siblings were awed beyond measure at seeing a magical whittling doll perform thusly. Soon their wonder turned to joy, however, and they began to laugh and to follow the cue of the older kids in giving commands and asking questions of the doll.

"Who has been a good girl this week?" brought the dolls stovewood to a halt and a quick pointing with the knife toward someone.

"Who has been sneaking around eating too many green apples?" almost always got the knife pointed at brother Bill and a burst of approving laughter from all.

"Can you make a doll bed?" was all that was needed to get the doll into high gear with the whittling once more.

Sometimes the stick and knife were replaced in the performing doll's hands by an old earthenware mixing bowl from Mama's cupboard and a worn wooden spoon. Then we kiddoes would chorus, "Cream the sugar for a cake," and the doll would spring into action, creaming the imaginary firm butter into the make - believe grainy sugar with steady, even strokes. And then after awhile when the 'eggs' had been added and the batter was soft, the doll would beat and beat, with overlapping strokes, 'round 'n 'round in such a cake - making, rhythmic way as to have us all start tasting a delicious warm cake straight from the oven.

"Who's sweet on Charlie?" from Nellie Sue's mouth brought the mixing spoon to a stand still and then got it pointed in my direction, bringing a blush to my adolescent face and a chorus of, "I knew it, I knew it," from several of my brothers and sisters.

After awhile *break time* was called and the naive little ones were taken onto the back porch for a drink of water from the dipper. Mama scurried from behind the chair and we teenagers vied for the enviable opportunity to entertain.

Soon we were into the act once more — enjoying the whittling doll, laughing, teasing. If Bill had become 'the invisible doll' sometimes the scene took a messy turn. All that was needed was for a statement such as, "You're an ugly girl." to be jokingly uttered. The doll then flew into a rage and everyone knew to quickly move to the back of the room before the doll began throwing her spoon, or knife — whatever she had in hand at the moment — into the audience. Then the offender would return the thrown object to the doll, apologize, and ask for a favor, "How about whittlin' me a good whistle" to appease the dollie.

If our fun lasted over into dark on short winter days and Daddy came in from the mill he would join in by making shadow figures on the rough smoked walls of our house. Placing his large slender hands at some location between the lamp and a wall Daddy made the look - alike creatures. Clasping his hands in one direction they became a dog and he proved it was so by adding the sound effects of a howling dog, one which had a possum treed down in the swamp. Then a change of position and the picture on the wall was quickly transformed into a horse, complete with neighing from Daddy. And, of course, there followed a long time of instruction as Daddy patiently tried to teach each of us begging children the shadow tricks he had learned from his father.

Or Daddy would entertain us on his juice (Jew's) harp, or blow good music on a comb. He taught us to do the latter by folding a piece of paper around a comb and blowing from one side of the paper, blowing up and down the comb for different tones as moving up and down a piano keyboard. If his lumbago wasn't acting up he would get up and buck dance while we blew on the comb, buck dance until little two year old Donald was laughing so hard he could hardly get his breath. It was a great chance for Daddy to tell us about his youth, about a time when he had won contests with his buck dancing and his fiddle playing.

If Mama took up her patching it was a time to grab a big button and get her to thread it up with doubled twine string. Then we would whirl the button and string for a minute and then began pulling the twisted string back and forth, ever so gently, making a humming whirr as the big button sawed back and forth on the string.

On Saturday afternoons now I see mamas dropping their offspring here and there — at the malls, the skating rinks, the video arcades — just to be free of them for awhile. I feel a sadness for them all, for the children, for the mamas missing out also. An aching for them to have known my Mama, for them to have been a part of my family when we bonded together in laughter and love. For them to have had the experiences I had long ago with Mama and the Whittling Doll.

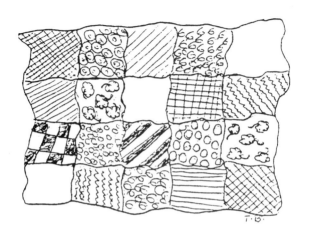

Old Quilts Are Fragile: Life Is Frail

Today I sat lovingly clipping from a threadbare quilt a few three - inch squares. The small, almost - sacred scraps must no longer be chanced on teenage excursions.

I thought of how the old throw, now reduced to absorbing sand and suntan lotion, had seen more glorious days. It had its grand beginnings at the patient fingers of my mother as she stitched it with love ere I left for college.

Because she was poor in material goods and rich in wisdom, Mama fashioned my cover with memories of childhood and home. In the center she used a scrap from a special dress she had made when I turned the magical sixteen. Here and there she placed pieces from my sisters' frocks, or from shirts she'd helped me sew for my brothers.

And in one corner she utilized a remnant from one of her own housedresses, a dress in which I envision her yet — cooking over a hot wood stove. And then, quilting the gift on wintry days in a half - warm room, Mama had the love to let my four - year - old brother slowly stitch my name into a square.

Oft in my dorm the quilted memories brought me an emotional warmth as I wrestled with my widening world; the crudely stitched "NONA" reminded me of my sweet little brother's tearful parting, "Now who's gonna make me apple pies?"

As the fading letters gazed up at me from my firstborn's playpen, word came that the boy - stitcher had been snatched from life in the bloom of youth. I looked that sad day at the fraying quilt and wept over the frailty of all things, especially of human life.

Today I looked for the last time at my old quilt and thought how it had been a good quilt. It had served as a chatting place in the dorm, gone abroad to warm newlyweds in Europe, made a pallet for offsprings, formed a bedroll for youthful campers, and now it was being dragged as a beach blanket. Destined to be discarded, I snipped the memory swatches from it and wistfully placed them into a book.

Finished with the nostalgic clipping, I took up the afternoon paper. It told of the death of my dear friend, Miss Ruth. Through the hot rush of tears I could see the ever - present twinkle in her eyes, her ready smile; I could feel the charisma which had drawn me to her since we met a few years ago. I could see her youthful step and spirit, and they belied the ink which today proclaimed, "84 years old."

The sad news was almost unbearable, thrust upon me in rapid succession on the passing of other dear friends, Mr. John and Mrs. Etta. Mr. John's quick wit and laughter were a marvel for his ninety - odd years. The remembrance of the childless Mrs. Etta's love of children, of the twenty- third Psalm of David, and of flowers — these sweet memories of the dear lady pass over me as a breeze in spring.

So today I sit and silently weep. My old quilt is in rags; quilts are that way — so fragile and short - lived. My dear friends are gone; life on this earth is that way — more frail and fleeting than even quilts.

Slopping The Hogs
A Reward?
NOT FOR ME NOR THE PRODIGAL SON

Picture this. School takes in. Teacher announces to class: "Those who finish work quickly and do it well will be rewarded by work on the farm." It's the truth. Youngsters in many cities are now being motivated to do their best in exchange for a chance to slop the hogs, milk the cows, and plow the mules. Just goes to show you how thinking has changed.

Take raising and feeding the pigs. The Good Book lets us know that even 2,000 years ago young folks were aware that going to the pigpen was no great prize; that the Prodigal Son was on his last leg when reduced to feeding the swine.

In spite of my love for pork chops, ham with spick - a - bat gravy, and sausage smoked in the smokehouse I, too, despised going down to the stinky pigpen. My dread of feeding the pigs stemmed, in large part, from the food they were given.

Now I did not mind carting a wheelbarrow load of good, clean corn from the crib down to the pen in the winter. Nor,come summer, did I object to taking the shoats the overgrown cucumbers, squashes, nor the hardened roas'nears.

It was the everlasting kitchen slop that I detested toting down to the pigsty. Current sanitation standards being what they are I hesitate to reveal that during the Great Depression my family kept a putrid pail either behind the stove or out on the side porch — a slop bucket into which we put all sorts of kitchen scraps and peelings, even dishwater with its lye soap. And twice daily the pail had to be toted down to the pen and poured into the wooden feeding trough.

Sometimes the chore called for climbing over the sagging hogwire fence to upright the dislodged trough, then pouring the slop while the greedy pigs and hogs crawled on top of each other, and crawled all over your feet, clamoring for the smelly liquid. One was lucky indeed to escape this ordeal without smelling like a pigpen themselves.   (Oh, to have had today's computerized system which conditions pigs to feeding time and reduces competition, aggression, and stress in the pigs.)

"Apt as not, that hog'll run 350 pounds, on foot," Daddy'd brag to the neighbor on a Sunday when they walked down to the pen; so I reckon the food we gave them worked. Well, the things we gave them, plus the things they stole, fattened them up.

I had a hard time forgiving the creatures when they escaped their makeshift wire and scrap lumber pen and rooted up our peanut patch; during the time it took us to drive to church and back in the wagon they robbed us of peanut brittle and parched peanuts for an entire winter. And I haven't forgotten the old sow and her pigs who riddled our watermelon patch one moonlit night; it wouldn't have done for some animal rights' activist to have seen me kicking that old pigskin following her daring escapade.

Looking back I suppose that part of my resentment of our pigs lay with their home, their manner of life; they just "lived like a bunch of pigs," as the saying goes. They enjoyed none of that today stuff of being farrowed and finished in environmentally controlled buildings. And Daddy had, apparently, never been told that boars and sows should have their housing built on well - drained sites. Wherever we lived the hog pen was located quiet apiece from the house, on the lowest, most moist corner of the property available; a place with lots of shade trees — since Daddy knew that hogs don't sweat and can't stand heat. Often it would be built near a spring so we wouldn't have far to tote water in the summer to assure that the hogs always had a mud bog to wallow in, to keep them from getting too hot, especially Daddy's overweight brood sow.

And Daddy'd put them up some sort of little lean - to house, a place that provided shelter from the rain and from the cold in the winter. And somehow Daddy's formula must have worked, because we most always raised healthy, big hogs for our winter meat. Of course then again the credit maybe should have gone to the fact that Daddy was a hairy man. Because, as the local saying went, "Anybody who has hairy legs is a good hog raiser."

Yep, I'm aware that much has changed in regards to turning pigs into hogs since I was a slop- toting adolescent. Why, even Mizz Orlena has had to stop saying that her little granddaughter is "fat as a pig"; what with the new formulas for growing more lean and less fat on the porkers it's now more apropos to say "thin as a pig."

And the most startling development of all

on the hog scene: the hottest fad now in the world of exotic pets is to own a little Vietnamese potbellied pig. To let the pig live inside the house with people, mind you. Why, I've heard tell that some have given them their own little baby cribs with steps leading upward. They can be toilet trained, they say, and taught to talk, "Oink, oink. I'm a classy pig, don't bite, like to cuddle, have no fleas, been bought with the price of $3,000, eat oreo cookies instead of slop." (I still say that anyone who buys one of the pets is getting *a pig in a poke*.)

So the current trend is to reward school children for their good work and acceptable behavior by giving them a trip to a local farm to feed hogs, milk cows, or plow the mules. And children, born in the city, are responding to the challenge like ticks clinging to a dog's back. But there's just one thing I have to say. On the day when they quit letting them feed the sanitized piggies the shiny red apples and make them tote the slop bucket down to the stinky pigsty — on that day they are going to see more rebellious youngsters and poor achievers than the school systems have ever known.

Hats Off To Folks
Who Raise Pulley Bones

Whether I'm enjoying my Mama's chicken dressing, my Mother - in - law's famous chicken pie, or the Colonel's old fashioned fried, I never take the blessing of chicken meat for granted. Living with Mama during the good ole days when baby chicks first saw the light of day from underneath a setting hen taught me to appreciate pulley bones and the work that's required to produce 'em.

It was not the easiest task in the world keeping hard - headed dominecker hens from stealing their nests in the woods where both they and their little 'doodies' were easy prey for possums and foxes. And once you had corralled the old birds and made them hatch their young in the chicken house or in a stable feed trough, there was then the worry of the hens becoming overly anxious as the biddies started to hatch.

When this happened the mothers would peck the shells off the baby chicks instead of letting the little fellows fight their way out, thus making themselves strong. In those cases, Mama would bring the struggling little birds inside and keep them in a box of rags near the warm hearth for a couple of days. Her remedy for premature chicks was the same as that used for chickens with the sore head or the dropsy; she mixed Watkins' liniment in their drinking water.

I will never forget the time my pet banty (bantam) hen got the sore head. It grieved me greatly to see Erma — so named after the lady up the road who'd given the young pullet to me — well, it made me very sad to see my Erma drooping around and not wanting to swallow the popcorn I had sneaked and shelled for her (because I was fearful the big grains of field corn might get stuck in her craw).

I was relieved when Mama said she'd put my ailing banty in a coop and give her water with some of Granny's good Watkins' liniment in it. That is, I had renewed hope until I saw Mama put only one - half little spoon (teaspoon) of that medicine into a full pint of water. I figured my

Erma was a goner unless I acted tast.

Seeing Mama then head to the spring with a big wash, I quickly emptied the pint jar of half its water. I then poured the remaining eight ounces of the liniment therein. Next I screwed the little serving pan - top onto the jar, shook it vigorously, and quickly turned it upside down as I'd learned to do.

I then stuck Erma's beak into the potent mixture which drained into the pan and I threw her head backward to make sure she swallowed the needed medication. After I'd administered this emergency treatment to my dear little hen several times I sat her down to await a miraculous recovery.

She began to loudly squawk and circle inside her coop at full speed. Daddy came running from the barn to investigate the disturbance just as I was prematurely thanking God for Erma's full recovery. At that moment Erma fell a - sprawling, threw her head backward, and gave up the ghost forevermore. Right then and there I started appreciating folks who raise pulley bones; it's a hard thing knowing how much Watkins' liniment to give 'em when they've got the sore head or the dropsy!

There were many other opportunities in my childhood for me to learn to appreciate poultry producers. I was reminded of a major one last spring when the local paper carried a story of a theft. Seems a couple were caught stealing cow manure. Now I'm a Saved - by - God's - Grace Christian and I believe God's commandment forbidding theft. But even if I were an atheist there are two things that you'd never have to worry about me stealing, thanks to my childhood experiences. One of them is cow manure and the other is chicken manure.

Now I know city folks in this day refer to it as chicken litter. But it is still nothing more than chicken excrement mixed with wood shavings. And, believe me, mixing it with something does not exactly take the edge off of having to clean out the hen house come spring.

I should know. Mama was a woman before her time and four, five decades back she had Daddy bringing sawdust from the sawmill to spread underneath the roosts in the hen house. And then when Bill and I were instructed every March to clean out the hen house and spread the takings in the garden — well, the fact that the chicken waste was mixed with sawdust did not appreciably improve mine and Bill's attitude toward the unpleasant task. The chore made us vow to never make our living raising chickens.

I've been surprised recently to read that our government has paid experimental agriculturists big money to discover that chicken litter is a "great fertilizer to use for growing vegetables." Well, my Mama took great stock in that knowledge when I was only knee - high to a duck.

And I could have told folks years ago that we were gonna run into the problem we now have of trying to dispose of too much chicken litter in too concentrated of an area. I paid sorely for the same mistake a long time ago.

In a hurry to get the chicken house cleaned out, get it spread in the garden, and to be off to my friend Jewel's house, I put the refuse about ten times as thick on my Mama's rows of Kentucky Wonder pole beans as I'd been instructed.

Lo and behold. Instead of a lot of a good thing being better — when the weather turned dry the beans burned to a crisp. They became brown, and died as a result of too strong an application of chicken manure. And then Mama made an application on my backside which I have felt, until this day, was too strong.

Now I know that computers and other innovations have made raising chickens a lot easier than in Mama's day. You take, for instance, the mechanical watering troughs and the feeders. Some of those feeders, I've read, can now even discriminate against female chickens. They let the roosters eat their hearts out getting ready for the chopping block. And they make the pore ole pullets, destined to become egg layers, they make them stay on a diet; some of them only get to eat every other day.

When the birds get sick, I wonder, will those mechanical gadgets put the Watkins' liniment in automatically, just the correct amount so they won't wind up like my little Erma?

There are some things you just can't completely mechanize. Catching those chickens from off the roosts when they are ready for the market is a good example. Yea — I know that today the poultry companies will bring trained catchers to your big chicken houses and they will turn on some fancy red lights. The latter permit folks to see, while leaving the birds lulled into thinking it is still nightie - nite time. But with all of these improvements I hear that catching thousands of chickens in one night is not what it is cracked up to be.

Actually my experience with catching chickens off a roost is limited to nabbing one occasionally, just before the break of day on a Sunday morning — one to kill and cook for the preacher's dinner. And to the times, after dark, when we had to grab some fowls from trees and rush them into the hen house to save them from foxes.

Even so I can still detect a couple of faint physical scars I obtained while catching chickens. One laceration I got when I surprised a dozing setting hen in a low - slung chinnie - berry tree — that is, she had her disposition set on *setting*. The

other came from a rooster's spur when I was
dispatched to sacrifice him as a Thanksgiving
turkey.

I have emotional scars on my life from the
chickens as well. Deeply embedded scars from
the humiliation of having fowls flap their wings in
my face and deposit their litter on my being
whenever I caught them.

My younger sisters Betty and Trillie — well,
they tell me I "don't know nothing," since I never
volunteered to help our neighbors' catch
hundreds of the birds for the market like they did.
They did it just once, and then, unknowingly —
right after mass chicken production came into
vogue in Alabama in the early 50s. "Were nearly
clawed to death all night long, plus the filth, the
stench," they say.

Yep, my brother Bill and I, **and** our sisters
Trillie and Betty, are all for a commendation right
now.   Having lived on a farm where
Domineckers, Banties, and Rhode Island Reds
were raised — and having learned the hard way
— we all want to herewith Take Our Hats Off to
folks today who make their living by raising those
delicious pulley bones for folks like you and me to
eat. And we're hoping the chicken processors will
learn to cut up chickens properly, so there will be
pulley bones galore, even sold in stores, for
pulling and making wishes.

Why, it wouldn't surprise us in the least if a

national study showed that the high incidence of teenage suicides today is tied to the fact that kids no longer have high hopes. They do not have the future outlook achieved long ago when we pulled pulley bones. When we found out by getting the shortest piece of the bone that we were gonna *get married first*. The longer piece gave us another great reason for living; it fueled our high expectations over someday moving from the tenant shack and *having the prettiest house*!

Peddlers Of Grit, Blair, And Rosebud Salve:
ENTREPRENEURS IN A DUSTY ART

Webster tells me that an entrepreneur is one who organizes, manages, and assumes the risks of a business or enterprise. My brother Bill didn't know it but he qualified for that big title at the age of 8 when he was selling *Grit* newspapers. Took an entire Sunday afternoon to get organized. Signed on the dotted line that he wouldn't let the dozen copies of the informative paper be folded to swat flies with unless the money was promptly remitted. Promised to sell the weekly news quickly and send in three cents for each copy sold.

And like any good entrepreneur Bill was recompensed for his management skills and his work. For walking, often barefoot, on the dusty or the frozen dirt roads approximately ten miles weekly, he was allowed to keep two of the five pennies that each paper sold for.

Don't get me wrong, Bill wanted those coppers. But sometimes he felt such pride in heading out with that little cloth sack with *Grit* printed on it's side until he would have peddled the papers even without the pay.

Bill was a great salesman. Usually sold one copy right off the bat to the letter carrier. And being at Mr. Eulie's little store on Friday e'enings when the sawmill workers came in with their big fat $10.00 paychecks was a smart move. It made my brother feel good to know families all over the community would, that night, hunker around the keresene lamp and read, on page three, about the calf that'd been born up in Idaho with two heads. And about General Eisenhower over in Europe.

While Bill walked the roads he was able to publicize other products as well. He'd mention that we had fresh turnip greens or sweet potatoes for sale; he'd be glad to run them up a bundle or a peck. That the blackberries'd be ripe soon if they'd be interested in us picking them a gallon or two. And sometimes Bill'd be joyfully waylaid on the road. The insurance agent would request a hundred red worms be dug for him or fifty big black crickets be caught from underneath the rocks and clumps in the pasture; he was bound to the Sipsey for some fishing on Saturday. All of these ventures meant a little ready cash for Bill or our family.

As Bill walked hither and yon peddling goods and services he'd often bump into others doing the same. In those days there were no governmental grants and free bureaus to assist small beginning businesses — none of the supportive services which are available in the '90s.

Yep, folks like Bill and our Aunt Lula had to do it all the hard way, all on their own back then. It was no wonder they both converged on Miss Betty Elmore the same day. Bill pushing food for the mind and Aunt Lula peddling nourishment for the body, *Blair Products*. Wonderful vanilla or butterscotch flavoring, and — miracle - of - all - miracles — a pudding mix in a box, either chocolate, vanilla, or lemon. Aunt Lula walked the countryside selling the products in her spare time, the time left after caring for a husband and twelve kids. She made a little money and got free products for her family in exchange for the hard work.

When Bill came home after a day of

selling, acting all out of sorts like he had something stuck in his craw — usually it meant that Walter had been out selling *Rosebud Salve* and had gotten everyone's money before Bill arrived with his *Grit* papers.

Believe me folks **would sacrifice** in order to buy that little tin box of *Rosebud Salve*! Couldn't blame 'em. True, the can wasn't much bigger than a little cat - head biscuit and cost twenty - five cents at that. But oooohhhhh, once you had lifted the lid it was worth far more. The salve therein was tinted pink, pink like the little rosebuds on our Seven Sisters rosebush out in the front yard. And the ointment smelled of roses, of fancy perfume more than being something to cure "whatever ails ye."

Whenever Mama splurged and bought a little tin of *Rosebud Salve* we had to be very 'savings' with it — a tiny smear over a wasp sting, a bit over red bug bites, an invisible layer over a bad canker sore. An older friend now confides to me that she was permitted to take a box of the precious ointment to school everyday, to use extravagantly on cracked lips or chapped hands. Another remembers that her grandmother used it in much the way youngsters use hair styling mousse today; after she had combed her long gray hair and put it into a bun, she sleeked the wayward strands from her face backwards by applying a small amount of *Rosebud Salve*.

Rosebud Salve was an ointment to the spirit of those who sold it in much the same way it soothed the body of those who used it. For selling a package of twelve tins of the salve one might get personalized pencils, and the young person who walked and sweated and begged until they had sold two dozen containers of the salve were awarded a Swiss wristwatch. Three senior friends last week shared the joy that they received thusly, wearing a watch for the first time in their lives.

It's true; long - ago peddlers of *Grit, Blair,* and *Rosebud Salve* were great organizers and managers. But most of all they, like my brother Bill, were willing to work hard to deliver products of the heart to neighbors and friends. You never heard folks saying such things about Bill as, "He ain't worth a red cent, always lollygagin' around, not worth his weight in salt." Nope, folks always bragged on my older brother, saying, "That Bill Porter sure ain't askeered uf work. Can do might night enythang. And he shore is handy when it comes to brangin' in a dime."

Mad Dogs and Dog Days
Hounded My Life

A rural rabies clinic was scheduled near our house. I announced that I was taking Mumba, the gentle Chow bequeathed me by my married son. Taking her for her rabies vaccination. My husband panicked, "Faye, you can't ever tell about those Chows, you're gonna keep on till that dog bites somebody, probably that vet or somebody up there at the clinic!" Now as much as I try to be an obedient wife I didn't flinch on taking that dog. I wasn't chancing it against rabies, not with my *mad dog* background.

"Yea, it's ter'ble when dogs git hiderfobie (hydrophobia)," an old gent who had his three coon hounds at the clinic mused. "Seen them dogs go mad a'many a'time. Jest git to slobbering at the mouth and running wild; youse better look out then.   They'se gonna bite ebberthang 'n ebberboddy in sight. Happens mostly during Dog Days, th' horriblest part uh summ'r. And then youse gonna be in terrible misery 'fore youse pass."

"Amen, Brother, Amen," confirmed another who sat on a little bench under the same shade tree.   He was holding a leash with a little brown-and-white beagle thereon.   "'Member when I'se jest a little thang. One morning old Uncle Joe he come a'running up through the woods, wide open, had his gun, a'running up toward our house and a 'hollerin', "There's a ma'dog on the loose!" Uncle Joe'd seed it out early that morning, out near his hog pen and it had skeered him might nigh t'death 'fore he could git his gun and head out atter it.

I was able to identify with both their stories. And I shared a couple of my own. Told them about the time when we lived up on Pea Ridge. There we were out in the field behind the barn a'working when Daddy suddenly stopped his mule, cupped his big hand behind his ear, and hollered to us hoe hands.

"LISTEN . . . LISTEN . . . SOUNDS LIKE A MADOG A'COMIN'." Unhooking from the plowstock, he shouted, "BILL TAKE THE MULE T'TH' STALL AND YA'LL RUN FER YER LIVES, GIT IN TH' BARN LOFT."

Then Daddy made a beeline for the house and his 12-gauge. We young'uns, frightened nigh to death, remembering stories we'd been told, watched from the safety of the loft while the tormented dog came into sight, running this way and that in a wild frenzy, its bark piercing the air and sending a chill down our spines. Daddy stood on the back porch and, as he later related, took careful aim. Then, pulling the trigger, his only shell found it's mark and saved both his family and his livestock from the terrible virus.

Daddy wouldn't let us near the dead dog. Wouldn't even touch it himself. Dug a hole nearly to China and just rolled the dangerous carcass in by means of his shovel. He filled up the hole, piled heavy rocks on top of the dirt. Then came to the back porch and scrubbed his hands a full five minutes with lye soap. Talked about how you didn't have to get bit, how just one little drop of that dog's spit could get in a sore or a scratch on your hand and make you go mad.

That day after the doomed dog was buried Mama repeated the following story, which we'd heard many times before and which I recently shared with the oldtimers at the rabies clinic.

Seems when Mama was, as a young miss, employed at the state mental institution she had as her patient a middle-aged women whom she never forgot. "A pretty woman she was. And sweet. But she'd been bitten, or so they said, been bitten by a rabid dog when she was just a young mother. Didn't realize the dog was dangerous since it hadn't gone mad, wasn't vicious. So she didn't go off to get the treatment. There is a treatment; abody can take fourteen painful shots in their stomach, one a day for two weeks, with a shot needle that's six to eight inches long," Mama related.

"But that lady didn't get the treatments and every once-in-a-while she'd go stone mad. Just go into a rage, start slobbering like a dog 'cause she couldn't swallow. Times like that she couldn't stand the sight of water, it made her throat get tighter; that's why some call it hydrophobia, or 'fear of water.' Well, the pore soul'd tear her clothes all off, we'd have to put her in the cross hall to keep her from harming herself and others," Mama'd continued.

"Then after a few hours the pore lady's misery would pass and she'd be calm for a few days. Course some said it wasn't really rabies or she'd have soon died from the disease, the way dogs do," Mama had concluded the day Daddy killed that mad dog, planting the sad consequence of a ma'dog bite in my mind so firmly that I related it, forty-five years later, to the folks who waited there with me, waited at the rural rabies clinic on that hot July Day.

Had my sister been at the rural rabies clinic she could have added her hair-raising memories of the night at Aunt Margaret's when Uncle Dock rushed in, shouting that no one should go outside the door, that a pack of madogs were in the woods near the small-town neighborhood.

Trillie shivers even today as she recalls the blood - curdling barks and howls of the dogs gone mad, running in a ferocious herd. And how she and Aunt Margaret and the cousins huddled with hushed breaths inside the house, listening as the men took guns and hunted down the dogs. Even when the shotguns and the howls were quieted, sleep failed to come, my sister relives that scarry night four decades past.

Two days after Mumba was safely innoculated and my husband Joe had eaten crow, I met with folks at the Oak Grove Church. Ina Mae mentioned a scratch on her hand and Cordie Bell said, "Well you know it'll never heal 'til atter Dog Days; they'll be over on August eleben, according to the calendar." It sounded for the world like predictions my Granny once made about Dog Days. Well, Cordie Bell's Dog Days' comment got the ball to rolling and folks started telling ma'dog stories to beat the band.

Brother Bennie told one following which

he and I both agreed the hero would've won the Congressional Medal of Honor had it happened today. You see what you think:

"The year was 1917. I was about ten. Word was out in the community that a madog was round 'about and all the menfolk were out with their guns, all out hunting for it. Only trouble was, they were looking in the wrong places. For meantime the kiddoes from that neck of the woods were walking the road together, heading for a day's session of summer school. They were just ambling along, the younger ones out front, singing and chatting; the olders behind, courtin' and what-have-ye," Bennie was transported as he talked.

"Roger, the short, stocky 12 year old, was passing the trip by whittling on a stick with his Barlow knife's stubby little blade. When suddenly on a high bank above them appeared the silent, deadly form of the feared dog, foaming at the mouth. The children froze in their tracks as the dog leaped onto the roadway below, leaped into the midst of the smallest children."

"With lightning speed, and not a thought for himself, Roger lunged forward and locked his left arm around the dog's venomous head," Bennie stood, locked his arm and demonstrated, breathing heavily as he relived that decisive action seven decades back. "Swifter almost than the eye Roger's right hand pumped the Barlow back and forth, each time thrusting the knife into the heart and chest of the slobbering, vicious animal who struggled mightily to retaliate. Roger did not cease until the threat had passed, until all life lay drained from that deadly body."

I came home from the Oak Grove gathering still pondering the story of Roger who deserved a medal. Ironically, that night the newspaper carried two stories which related to my family's feelings about dogs. The first mentioned that our good governor had proclaimed this the 'YEAR OF THE DOG'; Joe objected strongly because he still fears the Chow dog; I resented it because I have a morbid fear of rabies, the disease transmitted most often by dogs.

The second story told of a Hindu priest in India being gored to death by a rabid steer as the good feller performed a funeral. The fact that the Hindus believe the god of death rides on the horns of a bull from Hell seemed, on the surface, to be true in this instance. But, not believing as a Hindu but as a Christian instead, I believe that God is the one who decides when people depart this life for their destination of either Heaven or Hell.

Nontheless, the stories I've heard and my own experiences with ma'dogs make me lean strongly toward the opinion that a'body *can* hasten their own death and that of many other creatures as well if they procrastinate when it comes to vaccinating dogs and keeping them from going mad during Dog Days, or during any other days for that matter.

Nowadays when youngsters are walking a quarter of a mile to the mailbox their mothers will caution against muggers and kidnappers. In my day mamas constantly called out the warning to children, "Keep an eye out for madogs on the way to meet the letter carrier and back." I ask you, "Is there any wonder, given my childhood, that I have a phobia about ma'dogs; since mad dogs and dog days have *always* hounded my life?"

It's Fall In
The Country

I needed neither almanac nor thermometer to tell me fall had arrived in the country. The heightened aroma of the morning's coffee and the change in the wailing of the train alerted my senses. A glance at the outside provided the conclusive evidence. Lady Fall had indeed slipped in and put out her elaborate decorations while the soft rain fell on my sleep one night. Just yesterday the sweet gums viewed from my typewriter were pine green. Today as they catch the autumn breeze their leaves are pretty dancers in skirts of maize, crimson, and bittersweet brown.

The gums' barren trunks, summer's awkward legs, now appear brillantly stocking - ed in the mellowed sunlight. And pollen - heavy heads of goldenrod form the background of the stylish leotards for the gums. Then, joining them to complete the patterned laces are the royal purples and violets of the wild verbena and ageratum.

The persimmon tree up the road a piece is hanging heavy, expecting soon a frost to complete the ripening of its glossy orange berries. Not far away tell - tale signs reveal the 'possoms' reluctance to await nature's full term.

The wild animals also keep beating me to the few juicy muscadines which drop daily from their sky - high swing near the creek bank. I wish for my strong brother Bill to shimmy up the oak and shake the large vine, as in our childhood, bringing a mock hailstorm of purple fruit down upon my head.

I see the cows munching lazily in the dying pasture where only yellow bitterweeds remain in plentiful supply. I breathe a sigh of relief that I'm now getting my milk and butter at the store.

The squirrels who live in my yard are working themselves into a frenzy hiding acorns, pecans and hickory nuts like a Mama on Easter concealing colored eggs from keen eyes.

Aging hay balers chug across small farm

lands.   They, like the famed Little Engine that refused defeat, maintaining, "I . . . think . . . I can, I . . think . . I can, I . think . I . can, I think I can, IthinkIcanIthinkIcanIthinkIcan."   The tired old balers now spit bales from their gaping mouths, determined to beat the winter rains.

Here and there a few acres of cotton are still seen, resplendent now in their pure wedding gowns of softest white, just waiting like beautiful brides to be claimed by eager grooms.

Soybean fields are golden, almost ripe for the harvest. And last week I saw three men pulling corn by hand, tossing it into a nearby mule - drawn wagon, a vestage of by - gone years.

Mildred has invited me up to chat and pick peanuts from the vines. This neighborly gesture is but a flicker compared to the fall fellowshipping festivals that are currently sweeping the country like wildfire. Unable to wait for Halloween and Thanksgiving get - togethers, folks long ago invented high school football and county fairs. Recently they've come up with other excuses for socializing.

This year women are congregating by the droves at trade days, bazaars and craft shows. Some men are also straggling to these shady spots with their wives. But most males are sitting on little stools, out in hot open fields with the birds. Confidentially I think all of this flurry of outside activity is just a celebration of the lovely fall God has sent to the country, just a last - ditch effort on the part of parents to save their sanity, a welcomed respite between being holed up with kids during the stiffling heat and the coming bitter cold.

Killer Bees Don't Hold
A Candle to Picking
Velvet Beans

The news is out: The Killer Bees Have Crossed the Border. And one U.S. citizen has already been attacked by the vicious insects and left despairing of his very life.

It seems that every generation has it's thorns - in - the - flesh, has those things which abound to make life miserable. During my childhood I encountered more than one thing which threatened to wipe out my desire to live. Falling prey to a whole passel of stinging worms on the back forty was one of them. If Daddy had not whipped out his can of Prince Albert and made a paste in much the way that Jesus made a plaster of dirt and spittle when restoring sight to a blinded man — if Daddy hadn't quickly applied that nicotene plaster to my multiple stings I would not have lived to write this story.

Chiggers, chinches, and head lice also did their part to eradicate me from off the face of this earth — or at least to make me wish to depart. Pulling fodder on a hot day when the fuzz on the corn stalks irritated my body mercilessly was distress in the flesh personified. Add to that an encounter with several camouflaged nettles and you have pain indescribable racking my body, making me lisp prayerfully, "Swing low, Sweet Chariot."

But none of the foregoing miseries nor the torments that may chill the blood of future generations are even in the ballpark with the horror experienced from picking velvet beans. I am here today only because I picked just a precious few of them, picked one short time in my life.

There I was spending the night with Myrtice. We scarcely debarked the school bus when her mama directed, "Grab some sacks and a cold tater as soon as your clothes are changed. You've gotta pick beans down in the corn patch."

Picking my first few beans I was intrigued with the fuzz on the fat pods which felt cuddly like the velvet collar on the coat I'd inherited. I soon realized there was little similarity between the two.

The velvet I enjoyed made me feel snug, comfy, at peace. The fine fibers on the beans sent tongues of fire raging over my body, from head to foot, racked my body with insufferable anguish.

"HOLY MOLEY, CAPTAIN MARVEL," I cried. Then I abruptly announced to Myrtice that I was sick and had to go home. I quickly high - tailed it down to our spring where I bathed in the cold, clear water for a long, long time.

My Uncle Ferman recently told of a time when he and his brother Perve lived through the velvet - bean torture. Seems Ferman had picked the devilish pods before and knew what to expect, yet never "let on" to Perve when time came for them to harvest the legumes their Pap had planted in his corn.

They took two foot tubs to the field and, with Perve initially questioning the need of wearing the sock - gloves, "we dev in," Ferman related, and began the task of pulling the dried beans for the livestock. It wasn't many minutes, however, until the 12 - year - old Perve began to complain, "Ants are stinging me and I can't see 'em!" Ferman was stinging too, but he still never "let on." Perve's eventual realization of the source of his torture helped not in passing the time until sundown.

"By the time we got home Perve was cuttin' a rusty, was stangin' so bad he pulled his clothes off and run around the house till he found a tub u'water to git in," Ferman laughingly told of his deceased brother. "He jest pulled his clothes plumb off!"

"But we growed a lot uv em on that hill that year. Aunt Harriet had a little ole one-quart-cow and every time she went to milk I'd have to go up there in the loft and git her a handful 'uv them beans and a few nubbins."

"I don't like 'em much fer feed. You can have 'em crushed and they'll make good feed or the cows **will** eat 'em plain. But they're jest as hard as a rock, mightnigh. I heard tell of folks cooking 'em fer the cows; either way they're lots uv bother," my Daddy's dear brother went on and on, trying to satisfy my incessant yearning for long- ago lines.

I, too, have heard of folks cooking the beans for the cattle. Buna shared that every day her mother cooked a pile of the beans they had shelled. Cooked them on the back of the kitchen stove in a huge old pot. And the cow loved them.

Another friend shares that his family daily cooked a big black washpot full of the beans, hulls and all. Placed the pot out near the barn, drawed water from the well to put into it, poured in the beans and built up a fire to last a couple of hours. Stirred the beans occasionally, then cooled and fed to the hungry cows who, in turn, increased their milk output.

Never mind the differing ways the velvet beans were fed, it seems they were one long story of trouble and aggravation from beginning to end. From the time of planting when corn had to be up some size before the beans were planted by hand — by digging holes between the corn and dropping in the velvet bean seeds. Yes, allowing the corn to get a head start was necessary so the beans would not choke them out when they started scampering up the corn stalks like Jack climbing up the beanstalk. This entailed a lot of extra labor.

But the worst work of all was when harvest time came; for 'twas then the picking of the velvet beans would curdle the blood. The pain was enough to convulse you even if you first rubbed your arms, face, and neck with burnt motor oil for protection as some did.

I guess the hell - on - earth from bean pickin' paralled the week my Daddy once spent picking cotton in the Mississippi Delta. "Mr. Homans come and got a bunch uv 'em to go down and pick cotton but they didn't stay but a week, I think it was," Uncle Ferman filled in my

blanks. "That was Charles Homans' brother —
you know Charlie is the one your Daddy, Ira,
once boarded with down in West End before he
married Pearlie, your Mama. Well, Charlie had
two girls, Moatie Gay and Ottie Pearl. Moatie
Gay married a lawyer, I think."

"Well, I was too young to go to the Delta,"
Ferman spoke with a sort of relief to his voice,
"but him and Gray and Olen Hall and Tillman
Pugh, four or five uv 'em went off down there.
The mosquitoes were so bad they jest ate 'em up,
mightnigh."

"They jest stripped it, bolls and all it was so
rotten, Ira said. Said them mosquitoes were jest
like a swarm uf bees mightnigh. And some man
come along and told 'em they better git outta
there before they took the fever. They burned up
their underwear, they did, trying to keep the
mosquitoes off uv 'em. **Yea**, jest pulled off their
underwear and burned it trying to make a smoke
to keep the mosquitoes off, Ira said. They didn't
stay many days, though." Ferman ended with
emphasis on the briefness of their trip.

So today my paper is headlining the *killer*
bee story; folks are frightened over the potential
pain and danger of the insects. But after living
through, or talking with those who themselves
lived through, the ordeals of chinches, stinging
worms, and mosquitoes in the Delta my pulse rate
remains calm. Then remembering the un-

believable depths of misery endured by many while picking velvet beans my faith in humanity to withstand a killer bee attack is strengthened. For the way I see it, folks, a killer bee attack can't even hold a candle to picking velvet beans.

My Pine Straw Playhouse
SUPERIOR TO BARBIE'S DREAM HOUSE

Playhouses made of pine straw were the stuff of my childhood. They gave us kids a start in life that can never be duplicated by pre - molded Barbie Dream Houses.

Long ago my siblings and I had difficulty keeping our minds on our business during church and dinner on Sunday. We were chompin' at the bits to lite out for our playhouse down in the pasture. As soon as we finished up the dishes we were outta there, taking the tin plate that was rusted beyond use and borrowing Mama's old *bresh brooms* (yard brooms) as we ran.

There in the pine thicket we flew to work. Not realizing we were learning architectural skills we set to work on our floor plan: the front room would face east with a fireplace in the center and have windows on either side. There would be four bedrooms — something we had never known in real life but longed for. There was the dogtrot, of course, and the kitchen. We also made provisions for the front and back porches, drawing them off with a sharp pointed pine limb.

Utilizing the bresh brooms worn down to the nubs and our bare hands we began to quickly build up the walls, to fashion the piles of fresh pine straw into some order. You never in all your born days have seen kids git so carried away as we did piling here for the living room wall, skipping a space for the window, piling again for the wall, skipping a space for doors and the second window that looked toward our tenant - farming house up on the hill. Up there dreams often shriveled; down at the playhouse they all came true.

Once the walls were all in place and the spaces in between — the floors if you please — when they were all raked and swept free of straw or twigs, we began to build the furniture. The first thing built would always be a plump settee in the front room, something we wished for Mama to own. And we made two over - stuffed chairs like we'd once seen up at the big white house where the land owner lived.

And talk about beds! At least two beds in each of the four bedrooms, enough so no one would be sleeping at the foot of the bed when the cousins came. Big, thick mattresses like Granny's feather bed right after she had plumped it. And pillows at the head of every bed. Sometimes we took cowcumber leaves and laid them over the bed, like giant green fabric pieces making a counterpane.

We sometimes deviated from piling of straw when we came to the kitchen; instead we used an old piece of rotting board for the stove. On that we placed the rusted tin plate and the once blue enamel boiler which then had all its enamel chipped off but would be great for cooking twigs for green beans. After designating a bare place on the floor for the eating table we covered it with the very old piece of oilcloth Mama had reluctantly given up. My! as we stood back and looked at the place we were so proud it was hard not to feel biggity.

When everything was in place we were rarin' to play *playhouse*, everyone of us eight kids, from Frances who still played the mama at fifteen down to little Donald, barely toddling. Even thirteen - year - old Bill would sometimes join in: course he was the daddy and had to leave right after breakfast to plow or go sell fruit trees, like our real Daddy did.

And we let Bill make the big decisions, like whether or not we were going to kill hogs that day. We girls got real mad when he decided we'd kill hogs, we didn't want to be outside the playhouse all day, pulling that fat off the chittlings. And pretending we were cooking the lard out at mama's black pot. We now had a fancy house and we wanted to be fancy ladies, just cooking and eating and visiting with other ladies who came. (Besides, we saw what Bill actually did when he left pretending to go plow Ole Maude all day: we saw him climbing and swinging out trees until time for supper.)

There we'd be. Sitting all proper on the floor having a snack of coffee and tea cakes (the little cracked - up pieces of mud from a dried - up mudhole. These made especially fine tea cakes, or flapjacks, when the dirt contained a little clay so that it clung together when dried.) We'd be eating out of broken cups and dishes, left - overs from Crystal Oats packages, and having a high fallutin' time saying, "Miss Jones, how are you? That's a mighty purty dress you're wearing."

And Miss Jones would be answering, "I thankee, I got this bought - ready - made dress in town at the Yeller Front." There we'd be socializing in the most proper way when an old dominecker hen'd come 'a-traipsing her biddies right through our kitchen and eatin' place; we just couldn't abide it. We'd be apologizing high time to Miss Jones and chasing those chickens outta there with the bresh broom.

Soon it'd be time to call the hands in from the fields. We'd call and little five - year - old Doug, our make - believe hired hand, would come whirling up to the door on his toy horse, the stick that had a horse head sewn from a white stocking by Mama. She'd given Old Jim a mane from the yarn she'd bought to make a chenille bedspread and she'd added button eyes.

When Doug called wild Old Jim to slow down and tied him under a tree, he hollered in to 'mama' that he'd be in for dinner as soon as he washed up on the back porch. The Good Lord pity Doug if he got so excited he stepped over a wall instead of entering by way of a designated door.

And so it went. Sometimes when a young 'un was *play sick* we'd let them lay down on a bed. And heaven have mercy on 'em if we'd gotten a nettle in the pine straw pile. And, law, the time Bill thought an old rotting stump would make a good chair for the playhouse. He toted it up and then Nellie Sue sat on it for the space of one hour. As our real Daddy later said, "You never seed sitch a sight uv chiggers as the two uv 'em had that night." Bill just escaped death at Nellie Sue's hands by the skin of his teeth.

Playing playhouse, however, for the most part was all fun, something that we wanted to do every spare minute away from the field and housework years ago. It got in your blood and you never wanted to stop.

Two friends confessed to me just last week that they played in playhouses even after they were grown. Elsie said she was nineteen, married, and still loved it. Would go out to the abandoned chicken house where a discarded wood stove had been placed. There, under the pretense of playing with the neighboring children, she would build up a fire. Soon her husband's granny would come out and give the *kids* some dough to cook in the playhouse stove. Estelle's account rivals Elsie's; she unashamedly admitted that she played in a pine straw playhouse at eighteen.

If pine straw was not available young folks improvised years ago. Georgia says she grew up in Arkansas and had to use oak leaves for her walls and furniture. But nevertheless, she made a playhouse in the pasture and, like those of us who had pine straw, she had fun there.

Pine straw playhouses seem to be a thing of the past. But it wouldn't surprise me if a governmental study were to prove that lessons we learned down at the pine straw playhouses were the things that made us able to cope in later years.

Maybe those were the things that enabled boys to cope through WW II without going over the hill. And helped the young brides left at home to *hold it altogether* without jumping out of windows. Helped them learn about boys becoming men, and girls growing up to become good wives to husbands. Maybe it's the reason many who are senior adults today are tough as nails, have a good hold on life, are wonderful neighbors and great citizens.

Yep, learning to improvise, make do, get along with siblings down at the playhouse was worthwhile. Learning to cope with problems like domineckers in the kitchen. Or returning the following day to find that Ole Maude had laid down and rolled on the beds or done her business in the front room; having to clean all that up and start over again.

Alas, all of those great lessons we learned down at the playhouse in the pasture will never be learned by children today who have their playhouses bought for them. Pity the deprived kids whose parents just plunk down seventy - five dollars for a Barbie Townhouse with its plastic furniture already intact. It will never prepare them for life like making a pine straw playhouse down in the pasture.

Be Patient
On The Freeway:
Country Girls Can't Merge

If you're driving the car behind me at a busy entrance ramp, please be patient. A country girl like myself just can't merge. I'm really not to blame. There was nothing in my background to prepare me for hasty decisions. Or for rushing impolitely, headlong out into a constant flow of fellow human beings. I wasn't even tempered to regard my own life so lightly.

Daddy set the example for my hesitation in weighty matters. Patience was the only way to save tiny cotton stalks that were mostly hidden by thick grass after a May, June rainy spell. First you chopped a hoe's length of the mess — the grass, cotton, and all — off the ridge. You skipped a short space and then chopped another hoe's length.

Then you put your hoe aside, hunkered down out there in the biling sun and tediously pulled that stubborn grass from around the tiny cotton plants. Lastly you'd take your hoe and bank some dirt, free of grass, around the endangered baby cotton. If need be you'd take time to put the dirt snugly around the almost rootless forms with your bare hands.

Now the only way a'body can face up to chopping twenty acres of grassy cotton in that manner is to possess a calmness, a patience in their souls. A 'one - step - at - a - time, Lord' attitude. Or a one - inch - at - a - time plan, like I now adopt when heading into heavy traffic.

And I always sit there at the ramp, pumping myself up against the onslaught of irate drivers piling up behind me, shouting. I build myself up by rationalizing, "Better late than never. Better safe than sorry. Better them mad than me dead." Daddy'd be proud of my patience, I figure.

My elder who was slow in making decisions would vacillate over which size sweep to use for throwing a little dirt up on beans in Mama's garden. And he'd quibble over whether or not to let the mules out to pasture after a summer downpour. Yep, I learned from him to look twice before grabbing cotton bolls lest I slam my hand slap - dab onto a nettle or a stinging worm. The only thing Daddy never hesitated about was heading to the storm pit when he noticed "there's a cloud a'makin' over yonder."

And I, too, have one exception to my slowness. At the first notice of a sale at the mall I'm off — like Ole Jake would say, "flapping my wings faster'n a hummingbird with a far (fire) in his teeth." Or, as Daddy's been know to say, "like a bat outta hell." (OK, I'll admit it. Some of you who know me well are going to bring it up anyway. You're gonna be clucking your tongues and saying, "Tsk,tsk, she has not one, but **two**, exceptions to her slowness. Isn't it a shame she's not slow and careful about thinking 'fore she speaks?")

But Daddy did teach me to stop and think before making rash decisions, before *jumping into things*, if you please. This trait of mine is evident in the five trips it takes for me to decide on a new dress at the mall, the hour on a birthday card for a friend, and the thirty minutes on a bag of potatoes in the grocery store. This trait became evident at an early age. When we girls at school were jumping rope and they started 'throwing hot peas'. I'd just stand there — starting, retreating, *catching flies*, till someone'd lose patience, push me aside, and run in ahead of me.

When I was on Bill's truck wagon, flying down a steep ravine at the rate of l00 mph, and I saw a huge oak tree looming right in front of me — I could not decide whether to risk the gully and turn right or the barbed wire fence and steer left. My inability to decide quickly caused my head to split the tree in half — that ONE time I ever rode Bill's truck wagon.

I once thought I'd outgrow this handicap in my life; this fact that climbing a rickety ladder into daddy's barn loft as a kid never prepared me for jumping onto an escalator in a modern building. But there I was, twenty - two years old, in a huge complex, the E.G. Farben Building in Frankfurt, Germany.   The place where Ike had been headquartered after WW II. To get to the tenth floor without taking the stairs someone indicated that I should "just jump on the paternoster."

Now this paternoster was a sort of dumb waiter for humans. A contraption made of, as far as I was concerned, many large wooden boxes stacked one a 'top another. And this string of boxes made a continuous circuit, without ever stopping, or even slowing down. One was to forget about the deep hole visible down into the bottomless shaft if one stepped at the wrong second. I should not think about it and just nonchalantly "hop on" they told me.

Well, some folks could do it, and not only get themselves thereon but pull on freight as well, in the split second one was allowed before the box moved upward out of leg's reach. Not me — I'd stand there for hours, 'catching flies', letting one box after another go up, trying to find the correct moment to jump, aggravating my new hubby with my hesitation.

And there was the trip husband, myself, and an aged landlady took to the World's Fair in Brussels, Belgium in 1958. When Joe hollered "jump off" (of the slow moving circulatory tram near the Russian pavilion) both he and the old friend disembarked with ease. Not me — I kept trying to get up the nerve all the four miles back to the end of the line — which was the **only complete** stop made by the tram. (It might have helped motivate me to jump headlong from that dangerous vehicle that day If I had remembered that Joe was holding onto my billfold and I didn't have a red cent on my being.)

After walking for three hours, hungry and tired among the millions of World's Fair visitors, and then only finding my two companions by a thin miracle — well, I thought that lesson would teach me how to take daring chances on my safety. But it didn't help either.

As a kid I could never rush my hand in and scoop up my jacks when my ball was coming down again. I could never grab a cas'un (caisson), an old car tire, that was rolling wildly down the hill. Or a swinging vine meant to carry me out over the creek. And my simple county life didn't prepare me for today's modern world.

I gave it a try when Rufe's old bull chased me from the apple tree in the pasture long ago.. I scooted under that barbed wire fence in record time. You'd think if I could do that I could now merge into heavy traffic on the interstate.

But every time I'm coming onto the ON ramp I start remembering how those rusty barbs tore up my back and ripped up my pretty feed sack dress to boot when I lunged headlong under that low fence. So if you're driving the car behind me at a busy entrance ramp, prepare yourself for a long wait; I always freeze in a dead stop. We country girls just cannot merge!

Lordy Sakes! It's Time To Trim The Wick

Ancient drawings on cave walls depict man holding aloft a flaming torch. Such records tell us that man has long concerned himself with light to dispel the darkness. Today, upon entering a darkened room, our answer to the situation is merely the location of a light switch. When I was a kid it was a bit more complicated.

As dark deepened inside our unpainted frame house Mama'd say, "I reckon it's time we lit the lamp." The lamp was then carefully brought from the mantel shelf, the dresser, or the eating table. The thin glass smokestack, called a chimney, was lifted from the lamp and inspected for cleanliness. If it was smoked from the previous night it was then cleaned either with soap and water and a good drying rag or it was taken to the edge of the back porch — to prevent black soot from falling onto the floor — and it was cleaned inside by using a crumpled page or two from the discarded cattylog.

If a fire was already lit in the stove or fireplace a pine splinter was used to transfer a blaze from one of them to the wick of the lamp; otherwise a precious match was spared with which to light the lamp.

Not only were the hard - to - come - by matches parcelled out sparingly, the fuel — coal oil, or kerosene as we called it — was used thriftily as well. Lamps were never lit at our house until it was almost pitch dark; only one was lit in the beginning, one for cooking supper by in the kitchen. Later when outside chores were complete, supper finished, and children ready to do lessons — only then was permission given to extravagantly light the second lamp.

If my sister Frances and I huddled under our cover in the dimly lit room - across - the - hall, cramming for an exam after the fire had gone out in the front room fireplace and other family members had retired, Daddy would keep calling to remind us, "Hurry and blow out th' lamp and quit wasting th' kerosene; we ain't got money to burn."

Lamps lit to cook breakfast by on dark winter mornings had to be extinguished — by someone puffing down the chimney like the old bad wolf coming to huff and puff your house down — the lamps had to be "put out" before it was good daylight. And it was a rare dark, dark day indeed when the lamp was used during daytime hours.

One culprit that resulted in the wasteful consumption of kerosene and one which had to be dealt with quickly was an uneven wick. The wicks used in our simple lamps and our one lantern were like tightly woven one - inch - wide strips of cotton cloth. When purchased for five cents from the mercantile or from the rolling store they were approximately 8 - 10 inches in length. They were threaded into place in the lamp's lips and hung down, limply, sucking up the precious kerosene and taking it upward to fuel the small fire. When a wick was trimmed evenly and turned down just right a small, smooth light was emitted while burning only a minimal amount of fuel.

I can remember studying my books by the fireside when all of a sudden someone would holler, "Look't the lamp!" The entire lamp chimney appeared to be ablaze with uneven tongues of fire shooting this way and that, smoking like me and my brother Bill pulling on a *colby* made out of rabbit tobacco. Mama'd bolt to the lamp, hollering, "LORDY SAKES, IT'S TIME TO TRIM THE WICK!" She'd remove the hot chimney with the sock she'd been darning, and grab her scissors before I could blink. She'd quickly snip through the flames to cut away the uneven wick that was guzzling down the kerosene and creating the problem. Immediately the wick would return to a small blaze and Mama'd step to the fireplace and quickly shake the bit of flaming fabric from her scissors. But often the lamp chimney had been completely blackened during the brief malfunction of the wick; it had to be cooled and cleaned before being replaced on the lamp.

I've been with Daddy at the barnyard feeding the stock after dark when his old lantern wick would act up the same way. Daddy'd stand there rolling the wick up and down, trying to adjust it without snipping. When all else failed, however, he'd say, "Run t'th'house and git yer Mama's scissors." Then he'd come outside the barnlot, far away from the flammable hay, before turning the crank to lift the chimney on the lantern. After trimming he'd stomp the clipped bit of burning wick until it was completely extinguished. Cleaning the chimney had to wait; removal of the lantern's chimney was more complicated than one on a lamp and had to be maneuvered inside the house later.

When young children were ready for bed in the backroom at night the lamp would be carefully taken from the mantel where it had sat all evening encircling our family in its warm glow. Mama, Daddy, or sometimes the eldest, Frances, were the only ones permitted to transport the lamp from place to place. There was the danger of fire and being burned, but more frequently there was the possible disaster of knocking a lamp chimney off, sending it into a million pieces on the floor. It was a calamity trying to scrape up the money for a new one and terribly hard to do w'thout.

An acquaintance shares with me an interesting story of how her mother once made - do after breaking their only lamp globe. The lady, working as a streamstress to hold her family's body and soul together during the Depression, had promised a dress to a customer the following day and was not about to go back on her word just because she had no lamp chimney. She built a fire in the wood stove, put a quart fruit jar into water and heated it to boiling to *temper* it. Then she took a glass cutter (which the Grandpa of the family had used years previously to cut window panes with) and she cut the end out of the jar. Then using the jar as a globe on the lamp, and keeping the wick turned down low so as not to overheat and crack the jar, she sewed into the wee hours of the morning, completing the dress for a camp meeting come dawn.

Long ago I loved nights when I could visit at my Granny's; she had a wondrous aladdin lamp. It gave off such a brilliant light until I thought perhaps it was, indeed, magical like the one in the fairy tale. But an aladdin lamp had its problems. It required an unusual wick, a little round lacy sort of thing that was suspended above the bowl which held the kerosene. This wick produced a circular flame instead of an elongated one and had a short life, especially when a flame shot up. When the fairy - like wick appeared as ashes suspended in space there was no way to remedy it by trimming the wick; the expensive part just had to be replaced.

Once a friend gave my Daddy a carbide light on a cap; it was the most fascinating light I'd known other than the electric lights I'd seen in the stores in town. Daddy had to put some little rock-looking stuff called carbide into the little can attached to the front of the cap. Then into a second opening he put water which dripped onto the carbide and produced a gas. When this gas was lit Daddy had a real handy little torch out on top of his head. It freed his hands up for holding onto his double barrel shotgun when he hunted coons at night. And he never had to trim a wick.

When the pow'r comp'ny gave us 'lectric

lights, about the time I started high school, it was like a miracle — being able to just pull a cord in the middle of the room and have a light immediately. But then there was Daddy, standing outside watching the little wheel in the meter, worrying over where we'd get the $3.00 to pay the light bill every month, saying, "That wheel is jest a'whizzin', ya'll hurry and cut out that light."

Yes, 'lectric lights were wonderful but they changed many things. With kids then doing their lessons off in several rooms which had bulbs dangling from the ceiling, our family just never seemed as close. Before we had sat near one lamp, had all sat doing our figures together, studying our geography, learning about exciting worlds out beyond Pea Ridge, listening to Daddy telling us about the time he'd lived in exciting Miami. Somehow after we became modernized with electricity it was just never the same as when the entire family had sat huddled around one lamp and someone had hollered, "LORDY SAKES, IT'S TIME TO TRIM THE WICK!"

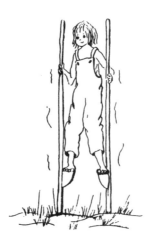

Santa,
I'll Take Tom Walkers
Or A Set Of Jacks

Dear Santa,

After hearing that your elves are having cardiac arrests trying to keep up with the new *Nintendo* requests I'd just like for you to know it's OK to skip mine and just give me some *Tom Walkers* or a set of jacks instead.

To be real honest with you, Santa, I'm not too crazy about anything that's like a computer. A young friend of mine worked ninety minutes last week with his *Nintendo* and just as he was at the highest level (I'm not sure, but I think this means he was about to win) — well, just then a young niece turned off the TV and everything was lost.

Remember, Santa, I had a similar experience in childhood. Several of us had been playing a game of jacks all Sunday afternoon. We were into our "tens" when suddenly a black cat ran among us, scattering jacks in all directions; we could never identify a winner — it still frustrates me after forty years.

You and I have seen fad toys come and go, haven't we Santa. In the last few years the *Cabbage Patch Kids*, the Voltrons, and the talking teddy bears have caused Christmas riots, only to pass quickly off the scene. And I predict that even *Barbie* and *Ken*, now into their third decade, will have a short life compared with the old timey, tried and true toys which I grew up enjoying.

Just to be honest with you, Santa — I'd enjoy getting some of those olden days' play purties again this year. Say, a set of *Tom Walkers*. And if your elves are too hard pushed to do 'em why not contact my Brother Bill; he could make terrific ones when we were kids — even when he had to borrow the lumber and the nails from the back side of the old barn.

Or maybe jacks, or whirligigs. Or marbles, the kind with *glassies* for playing the game of *ringer*. Or a Yo - Yo for learning how to do the Walkin' the Dog, the Cat's Cradle, Around the

World, and similar fun things.

A string ball would be to my liking, Santa. You know the kind made by putting a hickory nut or black walnut in the center and winding string 'round 'n 'round it all summer long, string that was unraveled from the fertilizer sacks. I liked it when we took a flat board and played ball in the pasture with these balls. Or used them to throw over the housetop, playing *Ante - Over* hours on end. (And we'd sneak and stoop to check underneath the house that was stilted on rock stacks. Check to see if the opposing team was coming around the house corner.)

Dear Old Saint Nick, I'd be thrilled over again seeing a Franch (French) harp or a Juice (Jew's) harp in my stocking top, peeking out over my apple, my orange, and my bunch of raisins on a stem. I might have a hard time learning to play the instruments again without my Daddy's fine example but it'd be fun trying. Maybe my brother'd wrap a comb in paper and 'blow it', finishing off a grand orchestra like we used to have back home.

Or a game of checkers, of dominoes, of Chinese checkers — even some home - made Bingo cards like my sister Sue once gave me for Christmas — cards which she had painstakingly made with crayons on pieces of a pasteboard box, using grains of corn for the markers. A game such as the foregoing would suit my fancy, Santa.

Or could you, perhaps, find me a game book with rules for all the old - time games like: "Granny Gray, Can I go out to play?"; "Bum,Bum,Bum, Here I come — Where're you from?"; "Red Rover, Red Rover"; or "London Bridge"? I would like to try to recapture the joy those group games brought into my childhood.

Santa, I know concerned parents are making you check a list this year, called the *Wise Purchase of Children's Toys*. So I've checked and all the possibilities I've mentioned meet these tests of good construction, safety, fun, and especially the test of time, of appeal for years to come. So, Santa, it would make my Christmas Day if you'd just give someone else my *Nintendo* No. 2 and bring me one of the good old things, preferable some *Tom Walkers* or a set of jacks. (And, by the way, make others' day by giving them my POT LIKKER, PULLEY BONES AND PEA VINE HAY book for Christmas, please.) Thanks, and I'll be leaving you and your elves non - fat milk and low - cholesterol cookies.

Our Old Fashioned Christmas Tree:

COMPLETE WITH TIN FOIL FROM THE SPEARMINT CHEWING GUM

Christmas trees of every imaginable color and decor are to be seen this holiday season. Having made their debuts in malls, office buildings, and homes on the tail of the Thanksgiving turkey they now swirl hourly on computerized platforms under computerized floodlights. They flaunt their expensive tinseled or earthy dress, designed by high - paid decorators, to the accompaniment of computerized music for weeks before Santa arrives.

Our Christmases and Christmas trees, when I was a child, were very different from today's high tech ones. I recall one specifically, in the late forties; it was exemplary of many others.

Seven days before Christmas, when school and our spirits both "let out," my siblings and I trekked to the backside of the pasture for the choice cedar. It had been discovered one hot day the previous summer — when Bill and I had trudged near and far, searching for Old Bossy. Over the last ridge we had found her — her newborn calf resting, like a gift from God, near the world's most perfect Christmas tree.

So that cold December morning when Dad was off to the sawmill for a little Christmas cash and Mama grabbed the chance to complete a few secrets in privacy 'ere the last hour — while our elders were busy elsewhere we eight siblings headed out. Big, dependable Bill lead the way, toting the freshly - sharpened wood axe very manfully.

As Bill chopped away at the ground, determined to get every inch of the gorgeous tree, our oldest sister Frances lead us in a high - pitched rendition of "Oh, Christmas Tree, oh, Christmas Tree, how lovely are thy branches." Soon we were homeward bound, singing lustily, everyone doing their part. Bill pulled the huge tree by the base, I brought up the tail end, protecting, carrying the precious point where the star would be joined. All others found a place, here and there, to lend their help — counting the cedar's bite as nothing compared to their joy. Frances walked alongside, carrying exhausted, but thrilled, little two - year - old Doug piggyback.

Mama greeted us at the front door, put her hands over her mouth — exclaiming over the tree's beauty. Then she threw back her head and laughed, "It'd be just perfect for the school house!"

After the tree made four trips into the side room — the room with the ten foot ceilings which doubled as a courting room for Frances and a bedroom for her and me — after grudgingly relinquishing one, two inches with each of the four trips into the yard the tree was standing upright on its wooden cross - piece made from a weathered board off the back of the barn. It's pointed top cleared the ceiling by one inch, no more.

Mama joined us for the decorating, saying how surprised and pleased Daddy would be that night. First the sweet gum balls were tied on — these ornaments had earlier been beautified by dipping them into the fifteen - cent can of gold paint. Then the "hikker" nuts were secured here and there with tiny sewing thread; these nuts had been camouflaged, wrapped tightly about with Spearmint chewing gum tin foil which had been retrieved faithfully, for months, from school trash cans. Soon pictures, hung here and there, spoke of Baby Jesus; pictures drawn and colored by small, excited hands.

The icicles — dangerous strips of silver metal cut from Daddy's Prince Albert tobacco cans — were next added cautiously by Bill and Mama. Then everyone had a hand in looping round 'n round the colored art - paper - chain which Sue had inherited from her classroom's discarded tree the preceding day. And the long, long string of fluffy white popcorn which'd been a family project for two nights was proudly added also. Soon the one short piece of red roping, the only remnant of our parent's city - Christmas the year after their marriage, — the tattered, but beautiful roping was handled and added with awe.

And yet the tree, being such a giant, lacked something. Mama remembered the scrap cotton she'd had ginned for quilts, which Granny Porter had carded on her last visit. So we gently pulled fibers from the combed cards and tossed them heavenward, permitting the tufts to rest at random, like softly fallen snow on the limbs of the pungent smelling cedar.

Each of us then scrambled under beds and behind chifforobes, bringing out one, two hoarded, home - made gifts. Soon they — in their wrappings of brown pokes, catalogue pages, or third - handed wrapping paper from the school's Christmas party — soon the prized secrets were underneath the tree. Then we all stood back in great admiration! "Surely, surely," we all agreed, "this was the most beautiful tree in all the world!"

During the six remaining days leading up to Christmas I felt perhaps I was the luckiest girl in my class because I was permitted to sleep in the room with the lovely tree. And I could see it late at night, after the lamp was blown out. Could see the silver icicles gleaming in the glow of the last embers in the fireplace — as the wind sneaked through the walls and made the strips of the tobacco cans and the tin foil from the spearmint gum shiver in the cold.

But when, on Christmas morning, I found an apple, an orange, **and a tube of tangee lipstick**, in the toe of the holey stocking I'd hung on the mantel's edge — when I found this from good Saint Nick **I knew, without a doubt**, that God had smiled on me more than anyone else in the whole wide world!